To Entice an Earl

by

Naomi Boom

Entangled Nobility, Book Three

To Entice an Earl

Cover Art by *RJ Morris*

The Wild Rose Press, Inc.
PO Box 708
Adams Basin, NY 14410-0708
Visit us at www.thewildrosepress.com

Publishing History
First Tea Rose Edition, 2018
Print ISBN 978-1-5092-1839-4
Digital ISBN 978-1-5092-1840-0

Entangled Nobility, Book Three
Published in the United States of America

Dedication

To my wonderfully supportive family
who always have positive things to say.
Thank you so much.
And to Brian—Go Dawgs.

Chapter 1

The humid summer night air greeted Alexa as she stepped through the balcony doors. The light of the moon washed over her and illuminated the almost empty balcony. Save for one other couple, they were alone out here.

She pursed her lips at the realization that now was the time. Now was the very moment she had waited for. Ever since her escort, Lord Edwin Rudgers, had met with her brother in private, she had expected a quiet interlude alone with him. And this was as solitary a time as one could hope, seeing as Lord Edwin had led her to the farthest corner of the balcony, away from the couple at the other end.

"Miss Farris," he murmured as he brought her hand to his lips. "I have anticipated this moment for days. Most impatiently, I might add." He chuckled, which sent a hot breath down Alexa's gloved hand, along with a shiver of apprehension along her spine. Alexa smiled demurely up at him and tried to muster even a little excitement for her very first proposal of marriage.

He ran his full lips across the knuckles of her glove and brought their conjoined hands down, not letting go despite the awkwardness of their position. A strange queasiness began to build in the pit of her stomach, especially when a gleam entered his blue eyes. He licked his lips, and she understood the cause of that unusual light. It was longing, desire even, and he directed his yearnings squarely at her.

"Yes, I worried this chance might never present itself." He drew her toward him, and Alexa complied, despite her reservations. While she enjoyed his company, intimate contact was another matter entirely. He towered over her, and rather than experiencing excitement at his nearness, she mostly felt intimidated, and not in a good way.

The softest of winds blew, and she shuddered. Her fine, curly hair had a mind of its own. No matter how hard she tried, it would never do as bidden. Instead, her locks came unbound at the slightest provocation. Standing outside was a tremendously poor choice if one expected her hair to remain properly coiffed, and Lord Edwin *always* expected perfection.

The light in Lord Edwin's eyes dulled as he considered a wayward strand of Alexa's dark brown hair which had loosened in the wind. With a scowl, he unwound their hands and caught the strand in order to repair her mussed hair. "Did we not discuss ways your maid could properly arrange your coiffure?"

"Of course, my lord, but a strong wind was an unforeseen hazard." She smiled brightly as she attempted to hide her irritation. Although her dark blue eyes likely betrayed the emotion she so wished to hide. They had a knack for darkening to a stormy bluish gray when beset by emotion. It was frustrating, to say the least.

He appeared too preoccupied by her curls to note her eyes, and she exhaled her relief. She had never thought to thank her unrefined hair, especially in the presence of the too-concerned Lord Edwin.

"And the face cream? You apply that regularly as well?"

"Of course, my lord." He had given her a cream from the apothecary to lessen the barely-visible freckles on her nose. As a gift, no less. The concoction smelled putrid, so she refused to use it.

"Oh. It does not seem to be working. Perhaps I can obtain a more potent remedy."

"I think we should allow this one more time before we try anything else." He did not always scold her on her appearance, but he seemed to express his concerns more frequently as of late, or maybe she just grew weary of his remarks.

Yet another breeze wafted by and dislodged a tendril of Alexa's hair. She scowled upward at the escaped curl and exhaled her frustrations audibly. Lord Edwin would never understand the struggles feminine coiffures presented, yet he still thought to instruct her. It grew tiresome.

She really ought to try her best to appease him but instead felt burdened with an impatient disquiet at his disapproval. His hand drifted back to Alexa's mane, and she hastily stepped back. "Really, my lord, you waste your time. So long as we stay out here, my hair will continue to behave this way."

Lord Edwin pursed his lips and tore his gaze away from her hair. "Indeed. I fear you are correct. I should have had more foresight than to bring you out here. I had so wanted this moment to be perfect."

Alexa raised a skeptical brow as he caught her hand in his. His dark blue eyes shone brightly down at her, and his full lips tilted in a welcoming smile. Everything about his outward appearance presented the perfect image, even the strongly chiseled jaw.

She shuddered at her use of the word *perfect*. She was beginning to detest that word. Saying he used it excessively was an understatement, and if he truly had wished for perfection, he should have chosen a better location. Not that the balcony did not suffice, but the air smelled musty, and the wind had toppled one of the flower arrangements which now lay in a wilted heap in the corner.

"I think it best we hurry this along, rather than allow something disastrous to transpire." He rushed on as he stared into her eyes. "My lady, will you do me the honor of becoming my wife?"

Alexa searched his face and her eyes came to rest on the top of his head where his own straight, brown hair had become mussed by the wind. Her lips parted in surprise at the irony. How perturbing that he should expect perfection from her when his own person could not qualify as perfect.

She almost groaned as she realized she had just used that infernal word again. It must be contagious. In the future, she would work on expanding her vocabulary so she did not utter, or even think, the word.

Suddenly, he coughed, and Alexa remembered where she was, firmly planted in the midst of the least romantic marriage proposal of all time. Her eyes focused, and she realized with a start that she could not say yes. She had always considered Lord Edwin the ideal suitor, yet now, his handsomely sculpted face and exacting mannerisms seemed exhausting to her. How could she imagine dealing with him every day of her life?

As yet another breeze wafted by, followed by

another escaped tendril, Lord Edwin spoke with patent impatience. "Really, Miss Farris, you will look a fright if you do not hurry."

Alexa stiffened. A piece of her hair stubbornly attached to her lower lip. She ought to remove it, but part of her wanted it to remain in full view of Lord Edwin. Her wicked thoughts thrilled her, and the corners of her full lips curled into a smile. She should say yes, despite her reservations, but she could not utter a sound.

As the wealthy second son of a marquess, Lord Edwin qualified as a superb catch, but this business with her hair grew tiresome, and the knowledge that he would disapprove of her every time she stepped outside drove the final nail into the coffin. She parted her lips to speak, but stopped as the doubts returned to haunt her. What if no other suitor surpassed Lord Edwin? He might not inspire her to the fluttery feelings her younger self often dreamt of, but he would do.

Wouldn't he?

Before she realized she had uttered a sound, she said, "Thank you, my lord, but I cannot give you an answer yet."

He smiled. "I completely understand, my lady. One should not rush such an important decision."

Alexa cringed as he led her back to the ballroom, passing by the couple who seemed oblivious to everyone around them. She hid a look of longing at the very obvious feelings the couple shared. In fact, their love cast her feelings for Lord Edwin into a rather unsavory light.

She should have turned him away instead of putting him off. After all, her very first season neared its end, and one never knew what the future held. If she did marry him, could she live with herself knowing she had wed the first promising suitor to come her way?

Her skirts swished with each step, and she eyed the fabric of her gown. The color reminded her of clotted cream, hence the reason she enjoyed it so. Debutantes were not afforded the luxury of bold colors, and rarely did she appreciate bland colors.

Her attention caught when Lord Edwin stopped their walk, pulled out a small box, and inhaled something into his nose. "What is that?" she asked as a mild feeling of revulsion hit her. Never had someone inserted things into their noses around her.

"Snuff," he said with an impatient look before resuming their walk.

"I fear I do not know what that means, my lord."

He laughed and smiled down at her. "It is a form of tobacco that only the most distinguished gentlemen use."

As far as she knew, he hardly qualified as a "most distinguished gentleman." Yes, he wore bold colors in the height of fashion, but his style did not appeal to her. She shrugged as he led her to her mother. Lord Edwin had some unusual ideas sometimes, and snuff counted as one of them. Surely, she would have heard of it before otherwise.

She spotted her mother seated along the wall and grimaced at the dark look her mother sent Lord Edwin. He did not deserve such a look, but her mother held very strong opinions sometimes, especially in regard to her daughter's suitors.

Or rather, suitor.

Aside from Lord Edwin, no other gentlemen

occupied Alexa's sphere. And why should she allow another gentleman to woo her? It seemed wholly unnecessary when Lord Edwin had an excellent pedigree and handsome visage. When he had shown interest at the start of the season, she had stopped looking for other acceptable candidates.

Why, oh why had she done that?

He led her to her mother's side and placed a polite kiss on the back of her hand. Alexa smiled and whispered farewell. His serious demeanor remained unchanged as he turned and disappeared into the crowd.

Her mother raised a curious brow and asked with a twinkle in her eye, "Well, did anything happen?"

Alexa nodded and whispered, "Yes, he asked for my hand, and I told him I will consider his offer."

Her mother gazed back at her with eyes very similar to Alexa's own. In fact, Alexa and her mother shared a striking resemblance. They boasted dark brown hair, stormy blue eyes, and a petite frame. Alexa and her mother had once shared the same measurements, but the start of the season had tried Alexa's forbearance and resulted in an overindulgence of sweets. The added weight had helped her gain curves, but it also caused her to feel grossly oversized in comparison to her willowy mother.

Lady Farris placed her hand over her daughter's and smiled in a reassuring manner. She whispered behind her fan, so as not to alert the nearby matrons to their conversation. "You know you can say no to Lord Edwin. No one will push you to marry yet, and a love match would be so much more preferable."

If her mother knew how much Alexa preferred a love match, she would never have spoken those words.

Especially if she had known of the one certain gentleman who held Alexa's heart. One unattainable, best forgotten gentleman. Since him, no other gentleman had appealed to her.

Alexa could only force a smile and shake her head. No explanation would persuade her mother to understand.

Her mother opened her mouth to say something, but Alexa interrupted her by rising from her seat. "I cannot. We will never agree on this matter, so please excuse me." She turned and hurried away to the retiring room.

"Miss Farris!" A friendly voice greeted Alexa as she walked amongst the gilded crowd. She searched the throng for the source of the greeting, until she spotted her dearest friend, Miss Victoria Cannis. Alexa rushed to Miss Cannis's side, ensnared her friend's hand, and led her to a vacant spot by the wall.

"He asked me to marry him," Alexa admitted.

Miss Cannis arched a blond eyebrow, which presided over a pair of large, dark brown eyes. She would have been a lovely girl except for an overly large nose. Her beauty mark above her lip almost distracted from the overbearing nose, but not quite.

"Did he now?" Miss Cannis asked, her eyes turning frosty and her lips tilting to a dour frown. She crossed her ankles and arranged her skirts in a poor attempt to hide her disdain for Lord Edwin.

"Yes, he did." Alexa brought her fan out and began to cool her face. The ballroom felt much too hot and smelled much too strongly of flowers. But what should one expect when multitudes of flowers graced every available ledge, corner, and crevice? "Please stop puckering your lips so. You look as if you just bit into a lemon."

Miss Cannis chuckled and schooled her features, and Alexa continued, "He is a gentleman above reproach and does not deserve your censure." She inclined her head toward Lord Edwin, who appeared in his element, thronged by an attentive crowd. "Look at him now. He could have asked any number of ladies to marry him, and they would have said yes. I should be lucky to wed him."

"Yes. He is handsome, but that is all." Her eyes narrowed on Alexa and she said, "I find it worrisome that you cannot see him for who he truly is."

"And who is that? And don't just call him names. Give me a reason for the accusations you thrust at him."

Miss Cannis sighed. "You know I do not have a precise reason. I can sense these things, and something unsettles me about Lord Edwin. I ardently wish you would give things more time and not rush into marriage with him. Your dowry is high enough, high enough to wed anyone, really."

Alexa's heart softened, and she admitted, "Yes, well, you will be quite pleased to know I told him I must think on it."

"I would have preferred to hear you tell him no," Miss Cannis muttered as she leaned back against the wall.

"I know." Alexa exhaled the words and turned her attention to the floor. The pristine white marble shone like glass, just like everything else in the ballroom, except for the flowers. Those were a variety of every flower in England. It looked like a veritable garden in here. Her head pounded in the infancy of a megrim from the overpowering scent of them all, which truly said something, because she adored gardens.

"Why did you not agree?"

Alexa exhaled again and swished her fan. "There is just something…off between us." She laughed to relieve the tension in the air and said, "Did you know he uses the word perfect at least twice in every conversation we have?"

"I did not. Is that the only reason?" Miss Cannis leaned toward Alexa with lips parted.

"No, he also obsesses over my hair. It must look—" Alexa caught herself as she almost used the word *perfect* and coughed. "It must look impeccable at all times."

"How unusual! What else does he do?"

"Well, if you must know, he speaks of his father frequently, gave me face cream for my freckles, and talks with his mouth full." She giggled as she heard her negative list of Lord Edwin. "I know they all sound like terrible reasons to turn away a gentleman, but they irritate me to no end. He even hurried me to give my answer to his proposal because my hair rebelled in the outdoors."

"Hmm." Miss Cannis tapped her chin. Her eyes twinkled with unconcealed delight. "You sound like you should have vented your frustrations months ago. How long have you felt this way?"

"I don't know, since maybe a week after I met him. It would not irritate me so, except I have seen him at least weekly for almost five months."

Miss Cannis shook her head. "Well, I am going to go out on a limb here and say you two do not mesh. Why not say no?"

Alexa considered her words. "I should accept. Where will I find a better catch?" Her eyes swung to a couple on the crowded dance floor. The pair stared into each other's eyes, their desire for each other obvious. The woman was a beautiful blond, and the gentleman was equally as attractive, but in an older, darker way. She gestured to them. "Just look at those two. Maybe it is just the comely that find love."

"Don't say that." Miss Cannis frowned. "We both will find love. It just takes its sweet time."

"That it does." And in an excruciating way. Why did a love match have to be so difficult to obtain?

Miss Cannis sighed. "I know I am only on my second season, and you your first, but shouldn't one of us have felt any emotion? Tepid warmth, even? Unless you feel something for Lord Edwin, aside from annoyance."

Alexa's head dipped down, and a modicum of heat rose to her cheeks. She had never admitted her heartbreak to anyone. Miss Cannis deserved to know, though. "I fear I have experienced the emotion at one time."

"What?" Miss Cannis said a little too loudly. She dipped toward Alexa, and asked in a quieter voice, "Why have I never heard of this?"

"It's a bit ridiculous. You see, when I was young I fell for a gentleman who never noticed my existence. So, I put him from my mind."

"Who was it?" Miss Cannis inched closer, her eyes wide with interest.

Glancing around, Alexa ensured no one listened and then said, "Lord Collins." A soft smile played on her lips. To think of him was forbidden, something she had sworn never to do. "I remember the first time I saw him. I might have been all of five summers. He had just turned thirteen, and had the lightest unruly hair I had ever seen."

She chuckled and pulled out her fan to cool herself. "I did not like him, but he spent an inordinate amount of time with my brother, who I trailed after mercilessly. One day, Gavin teased me in a particularly mean way. I don't recall what he said, only that Lord Collins took pity on me and made my tears stop. After that, I worshipped him. Until the age of fourteen, when that worship turned to love."

This was the tragic part of her story. The part which made her nauseous with embarrassment. She averted her gaze and whispered, "He never noticed me in that way. For two years, I watched and waited, hoping he would see me as more than a sisterly acquaintance, but he never did." She shut her eyes to flashes of her fragmented, tortured memories.

He never noticed the way her eyes followed him around a room, or the way she always "happened" upon him. For two long years. His inattentiveness had awoken her to a harsh reality. Not every gentleman she fell for would be her prince out of a fairy tale, nor would he want such a role.

Now that she grew older and more understanding of the world around her, she knew Lord Collins would never settle for her. No, a gentleman such as him required a different sort altogether. Someone who did not have an almost plump figure or who did not prefer to dig around in the garden.

"So"—Alexa smiled at Miss Cannis whose eyes had taken on a glossy sheen—"I have felt the emotion before, and I have also felt unrequited love. I just don't think I am the sort to inspire love."

"I am so sorry, Alexa." Miss Cannis bit her lip and shook her head. "Lord Collins was a blockhead…" Her voice trailed off, and she placed a hand on Alexa's. "What of Lord Edwin then? Does he love you?"

Alexa shook her head, and returned her attention to Miss Cannis. "I do not believe so. I think he admires me, which will have to suffice."

Miss Cannis shuddered and leaned back against her chair. "Well, we both know I don't like him."

They sat side by side for several moments in silence. The dance ended, and the beautiful couple broke away. Another gentleman approached the lady, but she continued to sneak glances at the first gentleman. Alexa couldn't help but smile.

The mood had turned dreary, so Alexa asked, "How has your night gone?"

Miss Cannis deflated. Her shoulders slumped, and she sighed a weary, unhappy sigh. "It has been the usual. I have spent much of my time by the wall." She brightened as she admitted, "Although a certain gentleman, the captain, asked me to dance with him tonight."

Clapping her hands in delight, Alexa beamed at her friend. The officer was a younger son to an earl and served in the Royal Navy. He would make an exceptional catch, seeing as her friend erred on the shy side and spent most of her night on the outskirts of the dance floor. "Did he express any desire in furthering your relationship?"

Miss Cannis ducked her head as a blush suffused her face. "Captain Grayworth said he thought we suited but needs more time to further our acquaintance."

"Oh. Well, that's promising."

"Perhaps, but I require more time to tell. I am hopeful…" Her voice trailed off, and her cheeks turned crimson as a shadow fell over the ladies.

Alexa tore her gaze from Miss Cannis and was met by a row of tidy black buttons on a dark gray evening jacket. Her eyes slowly made their way up the towering figure, past the waistcoat with the gleaming watch fob, to the elegantly styled cravat, and to the silver stickpin with a sparkling star sapphire at its tip. It glinted against his dark lapel and her palms dampened with the realization of who stood before her. Her gaze finally landed on his face, and she was left with a weak feeling of light-headedness.

Chapter 2

Lord Collins had not changed in the slightest since she last saw him. His blond hair still looked slightly tousled, and his blue eyes still pierced her in a way that made her stomach tense. No, he appeared unchanged, except for a slight hardness around his eyes, presumably from his own recent heartbreak.

She shook off the butterflies in her stomach and raised her chin a notch. He never needed to know the effect he had on her. She might die of embarrassment if he understood just how much she melted when she stood near him. "My lord, what a delightful surprise to find you in London. Have you met Miss Cannis?"

Not even the ghost of a smile graced his mouth as he looked down on her. "We must talk. Now." The harsh tone of his voice suggested he expected her full compliance. He flicked dismissive eyes over Miss Cannis, and then dragged Alexa to the balcony.

She kept her back ramrod straight as he guided her from the bright ballroom. His blatant cut of Miss Cannis was unacceptable. How presumptuous to think he could commandeer Alexa away from her best friend, and then be rude.

His arm felt like cold steel beneath hers, and she could only imagine what the rest of him felt like. She sneaked a peek at him to confirm her suspicion. He looked almost too well made. He had broad shoulders and lean hips. It all seemed terribly unfair, because he likely ate whatever he wished and never gained a pound.

He led her to the far corner of the balcony and swung her to face him. The balcony still smelled musty, and the same tipped-over flower arrangement lay abandoned in the corner. In fact, very little had changed since she last stood outside, except the one who escorted her here and the number of couples mingling outdoors.

She moved to put distance between them and looked up at his unreadable face. The last time she had seen him, he had stopped by to see her brother before he left for the country with a broken heart. No force could have lured him back to London, much less coerced him to single her out at a ball. She raised an eyebrow. While she could not help but feel sorry for his heartbreak, he had just openly shunned her best friend.

Her blood boiled at the thought of his treatment of Miss Cannis. "How dare you?" She employed a sharp tone, which she reserved for only the closest of family. While Lord Collins did not qualify as such, he still fell in the category of people she could take to task for improper behavior. She would never behave so confrontationally to anyone else.

Except her brother. He deserved censure whenever possible.

He smirked at her words, which only made her more infuriated. His tone sounded bored as he tilted his head and asked, "Have I done something wrong already? How tedious."

"Yes, tedious for me. One would think an earl could behave himself. Instead, you snubbed my friend as if she were some sort of pariah."

He shifted, and the light of the moon glinted on his sapphire pin. "I do not have the time or inclination to be set up with your wallflower friends."

"Yes, well, you cannot disregard good manners just because you feel like it."

"Yes, I can."

"Not at my friend's expense. I did not have some unusual design on matchmaking, you know. I just wished to introduce you as good manners dictate."

He leaned against the stone wall next to the overturned flower pot. His eyes gleamed with cold disinterest, and she almost shivered from his utter lack of feeling. "Either way, I have no desire to encourage some silly chit whom I will never see again."

When had he become so frustrating to deal with? She tapped her foot and said, "She is hardly silly, and she knows better than to strive for a match with you of all people."

"What is that supposed to mean?"

She smirked at the flicker of anger which passed through his eyes and levelled a frank look at him. "Just that you are far too self-involved for any sensible young lady to consider as a possible candidate for marriage."

"Self-involved?"

"Yes, self-involved. You swagger around, thinking all others are beneath you. Why, it's a wonder you even came here tonight. Deigning to mingle with us mere mortals must be quite trying for you."

He clenched and unclenched his hands. She could feel the vibrations of his anger, strumming through her, shaking her with its intensity.

Slowly, his anger drained, and he shrugged. "While

I cannot agree with your statement, I have to admit I dislike being here. I can only stomach so many grasping title-hunters."

His words were devoid of emotion, stated in a matter-of-fact way which made her want to cry. Lord Collins used to be such a light-hearted individual, and she longed for him to return to his former self. He had changed when Miss Ashford left him with a broken heart earlier that season. Miss Ashford certainly had been a title hunter, but that did not mean he had to disparage the entirety of the female gender.

She shook her head. No amount of words would convince him of his error in thinking. "Why are you even in London? I thought you were hiding in the country."

"I was not hiding."

"*She* broke your heart, and you responded by sneaking away to the countryside. That sounds like hiding."

He suddenly appeared quite menacing. "You have no right to speak to me like that."

Lord, he looked even more handsome when irritated. He had a way of sidetracking her, and she mentally shook herself to regain her bearings. "Of course I do. You escorted me to several events earlier this season as an excuse to see her." Her voice quieted, and she leaned toward him. "You chose a terrible woman who almost ruined all my chances at marrying well. Therefore, I can say what I want."

Lord Collins had almost married Miss Ashford, but when Miss Ashford erroneously decided more brewed than mere friendship between Alexa and Lord Collins, she tried to ruin Alexa. Hence, the reason Alexa felt justified in her anger.

"From what I hear, you have been doing quite well this season, despite whispers of you being a bastard."

She gasped. "Be quiet!" Her eyes darted from couple to couple until she determined no one had heard. The rumor of her illegitimacy originated from Miss Ashford. In fact, that was the precise rumor she spread to disparage Alexa. "My life might have been ruined because of your lady love. Pardon me if I am a bit bitter."

He smirked. "Let me offer my sincerest apology. While I suffered a broken heart, your suffering was obviously far superior."

"Thank you." She ignored his sarcasm. "Now then, you owe Miss Cannis an apology, unless someone saw your very obvious snub, and then you owe her much more."

"I am sure no one noticed," he said with a dismissive wave of his hand.

He was an uncaring oaf tonight. Hardly the gentleman so renowned for his way with women. Alexa opened her mouth to chastise him further, but he interrupted her. "You haven't accepted Lord Edwin's proposal, have you?"

She stilled at his words. How did he know about Lord Edwin, and why would he care? A gust of cooling wind accompanied his words, followed by the inevitable escaping tendrils from her coiffure. She allowed her hair to fly about her and lifted her gaze to his. "And if I have? Gavin already gave his blessing."

No trace of emotion flickered through his icy eyes. "That occurred before he left for the country, and before he asked me to watch out for you."

Alexa had forgotten her brother's planned departure from London. Gavin and Laura had decided to adjourn to the country well before the arrival of their first child. "Shouldn't Mother be enough of a chaperone?"

He lifted his brow in question. "Would I have come if Gavin thought so?"

"I suppose not, although we both know she is more than adequate."

"Maybe, but I owe Gavin a favor." He made a short, mocking bow and said, "So here I am, performing my duty as requested."

No part of her enjoyed being viewed as a duty, not by Lord Collins. "I appreciate your concern over my matrimonial prospects, but I already have permission to marry Lord Edwin." She smirked as a thrill ran through her at her open defiance.

"That permission is no longer valid. Now, you require mine, and I am not sure I wish to give it."

She inhaled and stepped up to him. He was so tall, at least five inches taller than her, yet she would not allow him to intimidate her, not this gentleman she used to pester as a little girl. She peered up at him and planted her fists on her hips. "You cannot possibly imagine I would listen to you, can you?"

His eyes narrowed, and he straightened from his position against the wall which brought him that much closer to her. "I don't only imagine. I know you will listen to me. You have no other options."

"Of course I do."

"No, you do not."

Their gazes locked, and everything around Alexa faded away, except for the brilliant blue eyes which held her riveted in place. She brought her palm to her chest to make sure her heart still beat.

It did, just barely.

She finally broke away and whispered, "I have not given him a response yet."

His responding smile lacked warmth, and he appeared to gloat as he said, "Excellent. I never have liked Lord Edwin and cannot fathom why you do."

"I happen to be very much in love with him." She colored. She had just told Lord Collins she loved Lord Edwin. Where was her fan when she needed it most? Next to Miss Cannis where she had forgotten it. And now, she had to endure a most frustrating conversation where she admitted a falsehood. Not a simple falsehood, either. One which competed with the largest untruths of her life.

Her rushed denial teetered on her lips as a stronger gust of wind tore through her hair, causing several more strands to dislodge. She muttered a curse and reached up to repair the damage the wind had made.

His large, warm hand shot out and stopped her. The humid night air could not compare to the warmth of his hand on hers, nor could it compete with the spasmodic tingles breaking out throughout her body.

The contact was too unexpected.

Too intimate.

Too much.

She darted a hesitant glance his way where he quickly masked a warm look and took a step away from her. "Leave your hair."

She swayed from the loss of his touch and the lack of warmth in his tone.

"Are you quite all right?" he asked with a sneer, as

if to erase all touches of warmth with harshness. It hadn't worked, though. She knew better.

Whatever strange demon had overtaken him tonight was not normal and was, quite frankly, vexing to deal with. "I see you can choose to employ good manners when you wish."

His countenance darkened and he lifted a brow. "You evidently are just fine."

"No, I am not fine." Her cheeks heated as she realized what she had just said. Why couldn't she keep her mouth shut?

He stared at her and then asked, "Is there some way I can aid you, then?"

She swallowed. Now, she had to make up an excuse to cover for her rash mouth. "I just need to catch my breath."

"You are winded? From what?"

From your presence. She couldn't say that out loud, of course. "I simply experienced a bout of nerves."

"You don't have bouts of nerves."

"Of course I do!" He knew her too well. "The life of a debutante is quite taxing."

"Uh-huh." His dubious frown failed to reassure her. "Or is it the company you have kept as of late?"

"What do you mean by that?"

"I mean Lord Edwin would drive anyone to experience hysterics, much less a bout of nerves."

"You act as if you know him intimately. If anything, his character relaxes me the same as a cup of warm milk does before retiring for the evening."

He grinned. "So, he bores you to the point of sleepiness?"

Alexa scowled at his mocking tone. She ought to think thoughts through before speaking. "Of course not. I meant he does not induce hysterics, or nerves, or anything of the sort. He is the ideal gentleman for me, one that makes me comfortable."

He did not look convinced. "You could never be happy in such a union."

"Yes, well, I hardly need your approval."

"Of course you do."

She jerked her gaze from his. She began to count to ten in her head. Otherwise, she would have resorted to calling Lord Collins inappropriate names.

A soft, fluttering breeze floated by right as she reached the count of five, and this time, when her hair dislodged in the wind, she welcomed the distraction it presented. Now she had an excellent excuse to forget him. So, she ignored the gentleman before her and smoothed back her hair.

"Your hair looks better in disarray, you know."

So much for ignoring him. Her cheeks heated, and her lips parted. He leaned back against the stone wall without betraying a trace of emotion. "You act surprised. Has Lord Edwin failed to mention that to you?"

"He holds the opposite opinion as you, my lord."

"And whose opinion holds more merit? Mine? Or Lord Edwin's?"

"Obviously, Lord Edwin's, because he is the one I shall wed."

The light in his eyes dimmed, and he shook his head. "Yes, I suppose you should answer that way. But Lord Edwin does not value women as he ought, which gives me pause. Does he love you? Does he approve of you?"

They had never spoken of love but as for his approval, well, he must. Otherwise, why would he pursue her? She had already claimed to love Lord Edwin, so she might as well continue with the charade. "Of course he does. Why, he has given me some of the most thoughtful gifts."

"Oh?" He quirked his brow in question.

She scrambled to think of something he had bestowed upon her aside from that dreadful face cream. Unfortunately, she could produce nothing. "Yes." That would have to do.

The moon seemed to emphasize the blue of his eyes, giving him an ethereal attractiveness. He searched her eyes in the darkness and then straightened. "I do not believe you. About anything. You could never be so foolish as to fall for him."

She couldn't get angry with him for that statement, but her lie dictated she must. She gasped, rather convincingly if she were to judge, and then stated, "Only a complete lackwit would not fall for him."

The wind blew strongly, and he grinned. She was caught off guard, both by the wind and his sudden smile. "So, you are a fool if you love him, but a lackwit if you do not? Which is worse, I wonder?"

She exhaled and said softly, "I think lacking intelligence is vastly preferable to foolish. They do say ignorance is bliss."

He appeared unconvinced by her argument. "But you are not lacking in intelligence, and I never considered you foolish. At least, not till now."

"And what if you are the erroneous one? What if you are wrong about Lord Edwin?"

"That's the thing." He smirked. "I'm not."

Her jaw dropped at his conceited attitude. "Yet I think you are wrong."

"Then you will have to convince me, because I am more than prepared to send him away rather than allow his courtship of you. And I *will* send him away if I deem necessary."

And therein lay the crux of the matter. He held sway over whom she married, and ironically enough, the man she sparred with was the one man to ever stir romantic inklings within her. Alexa turned away from him. She placed a hand on the cold balcony railing and looked at the full moon above. "You will do no such thing." But she knew he would, and she would be powerless to stop him.

His voice softened to a whisper, and he joined her at the railing. "The girl I knew would not settle, no matter how easy it might have been."

She closed her eyes against the glare of the moon, wishing with all her might she could return in time and take back her lie. "Lord Edwin is hardly settling, and you cannot compare our childhood competitions to marriage."

"Can't I?"

Infuriating man. She pried her lids open and craned her head to spear him with a hostile look. "Of course not, and we both know you allowed me to win as a child. You were what? Sixteen? And I was all of eight. Of course I did not beat you honestly."

He smiled the first true smile she had seen tonight as he reflected on the past. "You had the cutest curly pigtails. I couldn't bear to see you sad."

"And now you can? Thank you." He grinned, and

she glared. "Believe me or not, I love Lord Edwin, and I shall marry him."

She traced the iron railing with her finger and enjoyed the pleasant breeze on the night air. It was a welcome distraction from him. She tilted her head back a little and inhaled. The faintest scent of roses permeated through the mustiness of the balcony. It was the one good thing about this confrontation with Lord Collins.

He lifted his hand to rest a mere inch from her own, and she eyed it. If she brought her hand to touch his, would she receive the same sort of jolting feeling she felt earlier when he ensnared her hand with his? She shook her head. She did not want to know.

He surveyed the darkness before them and asked, "You do not truly feel something for him, do you?"

He still had not bothered to look at her, so she took a moment to admire his profile. The moon managed to cast enough of a glow to set off his features, and even from this vantage point, he was without compare.

The silence between them stretched. The hole she dug grew steadily deeper with every falsehood she uttered. Her rational side screamed at her to tell the truth, but the way he swooped in and claimed mastery over her life made her wish to rebel.

"I do."

He straightened from the railing and turned to her. "That is unfortunate. I will consider his suit for your sake, and you *will* abide by my decision."

Her expression must have struck him as defiant, because he scowled and said, "I would not advise you to test me, either."

His tone held a warning which made Alexa freeze.

She felt guilty for deceiving him, but his egotistical nature lessened her guilt. Her heart stuttered back to life, and with her renewed vigor, a desire to test him emerged. "I will prove you wrong about Lord Edwin, and you will eat your words."

"You won't, but if by some miracle you did, you would receive Lord Edwin as your prize." He scoffed. "And he is hardly worth the effort."

That much, she could agree with. Just not aloud.

So, she raised a haughty brow, turned on her heel, and left him standing in her wake, looking very much like a fallen angel bathed in unholy moonlight.

Chapter 3

Maxon exhaled his pent-up anger as her alluring figure disappeared into the ballroom. She had changed so much since the last time he'd seen her. A new worldliness circled her that she must have acquired with the season, one which beckoned to him. She no longer appeared the innocent country girl, rather a woman in definite need of a husband to keep her from danger.

Danger such as himself.

He frowned as the wind hit him once more. He wasn't sure what had overcome him, but when her hair flew wildly about her, he had wanted to touch her. To pull her to him and kiss away the hostility from her thunderous eyes. The nagging voice of common sense had intervened before he followed through with his final wish, but even the slight touch he administered was too much.

He departed the balcony and almost cursed when the warm air of the ballroom hit him. Ballrooms were the worst. No matter how many flowers occupied the space, the room always ended up smelling like human body odor. The two scents fought each other, and he inevitably ended up with a headache.

He paused as he caught sight of Alexa beside her mother. Her curls glinted in the candlelight, but even more noteworthy was the way her gown accentuated her curves. Sculptors dreamed of such proportions.

How and when had she managed to acquire them? He should not find her appealing, but then, what did it harm if he found Alexa attractive? He would never pursue her. No, she belonged with a sweet, young gentleman who would shower her with poetry and flowers. Not he and certainly not Lord Edwin.

Lord Edwin.

He frowned. When he had first read the missive from Gavin instructing him to watch over Alexa, he had scoffed at the notion that she might marry. He had never thought of her as anything more than the little girl that used to pester him as a boy. Evidently, she had grown, and he could now understand why Gavin enlisted his aide. She was just the sort a reprobate would trick into marriage.

"I thought I saw you in attendance, my lord."

The sugary-sweet voice of a young lady floated to Maxon's ears, and he turned to find Miss Watercrest at his elbow. Her blond curls framed her face, which tilted up to him invitingly. This was one marriage-minded miss he would do well to avoid.

He bowed over her hand and greeted her, trying to convey his desire to keep their visit short by using clipped words and an indifferent look. "How good to see you, Miss Watercrest. I hope you have a good evening."

He turned, but her dainty hand caught his sleeve. His eyes went to her hand and he raised his brow, but she ignored his silent rebuke by giggling and saying, "Now, my lord, I had hoped we might dance."

Maxon started in surprise at her forward suggestion. Ladies did not ask gentlemen to dance. Ever. He might have considered giving her the cut direct for her impertinence, but Alexa's accusation forced him to reconsider. He would not prove Alexa right by shunning two ladies in one night, no matter how unintentional the first.

"Very well," he said, taking her elbow and leading her to the dance floor.

"I was so delighted to hear you had chosen not to pursue the Duchess of Waking. She was not good enough for you, and now you can discover someone more accomplished. Someone like me, for instance." She batted her eyelashes, and he swallowed his nausea. The chit thought highly of herself judging by the self-satisfied look on her face. Luckily, he did not need to look at her, as the quadrille started and the dance mandated he stand beside her.

He remained impassive, and she inclined her head to him. "I haven't given offense, have I? I had assumed you would appreciate the news of her recent marriage."

For the life of him, he could not figure out who she spoke of. He had never courted a miss-turned-duchess. The only lady he pursued in recent memory was Miss Ashford, and she was locked away in the country. "To whom do you refer?" he asked, not caring to hide his annoyance with Miss Watercrest.

He exchanged partners, but when Miss Watercrest returned to his side, she had her head cocked at an angle with a speculative gleam in her eyes that Maxon did not appreciate. "You have heard the news, haven't you?" She tittered and leaned toward him, making sure he had a clear view of her impressive bosom. "Miss Ashford is now a duchess."

Maxon kept his surprise from showing by pretending he had a sudden interest in the crowd around them. How could Miss Ashford move on so quickly? She had expressed her desire to be with him several times, but now she had wed.

A duke.

What a title-hungry twit.

The silence stretched before he exchanged partners once more. When Miss Watercrest rejoined him, he smiled and nodded. "Of course I heard the news of her marriage, and I could not be happier for her good fortune."

She looked disappointed but recovered quickly. "I thought you must know. It is all anyone speaks of." She sighed dramatically and looked up at him with wide, innocent eyes. "I do wish people would cease their gossiping. It is so very gauche."

He gave a noncommittal response and remained silent for the rest of the dance, despite her numerous attempts to engage him. Nothing would move him to spare the chit another glance, not even if her gown turned translucent. Well, maybe then, but only a peek. He did, after all, enjoy the female form.

He kept his attention elsewhere, while his mind sorted through Miss Watercrest's interesting tidbit. His courtship of the newly minted duchess had been well known, and when he departed for the country, everyone speculated as to why. Some thought she had thrown him over, while others assumed he had compromised her. He personally preferred the latter option, but now that she was a duchess, they would assume the former. If it weren't for the fact that he had ended their courtship because of her intolerable actions, he might question matters himself. She had moved on so quickly. Too quickly.

The dance ended, and he led Miss Watercrest to her mother. He searched the crowd for some older, married ladies. He did not need to deal with more of the untouched misses this evening. Debutantes were best avoided. Especially in his present mood. He had always behaved the consummate gentleman, but he was tired of it. Tired of all the tedious pleasantries that meant nothing. Tired of avoiding solitary interludes with ladies interested in trapping him in dreaded matrimony.

Yes, he was tired, but he would muster the energy to ensure Alexa did not succumb to an unworthy suitor. Even now she clung to Lord Edwin's arm, and judging by the look on the bastard's face, he returned her feelings tenfold.

The idea that she had grown into a young lady still shocked him to the core. It was as if she had blossomed overnight, into a woman capable of love. For Lord Edwin, no less. While Maxon had not kept tabs on the gentleman, he could remember Edwin from the schoolroom. Back then, Edwin was an obnoxious bully. He could not have grown into a likable fellow, right?

Suddenly, Maxon wasn't so sure. And to break apart a love match would require complete justification that he do the right thing.

He crossed the crowded ballroom and approached a harmless enough widow. She smiled at him, and he allowed a return smile to grace his lips. He would dance for a little while longer, and then go to his clubs. His pipe and a few glasses of scotch sounded like the perfect finish to a distasteful day.

****

The following evening found Alexa once more in attendance at a ball. She wore pristine white, which set off her fair complexion and darker hair to perfection. She might look her best in innocent colors, but they made her blend in with every other unmarried lady.

"You look marvelous tonight," Lord Edwin offered as he led her to the dance floor.

"Thank you." She smiled at him as they took their positions. "I do long for the day I can wear brighter colors."

"Why?" His brow furrowed. "Darker colors would age you."

She froze. Sometimes, a gentleman ought to keep his opinions to himself.

She couldn't tell him that, though, so instead of responding, she pasted a demure smile on her face. The orchestra started the set, and Alexa focused on her steps.

Normally, she didn't favor dancing, but the activity did seem more enjoyable with Lord Edwin leading her. The intricacy of the movements only emphasized his prowess as she passed from one partner to the next. None of the other gentlemen had the finesse of Lord Edwin nor the ability to make her feel as though she floated.

Small talk, on the other hand, proved taxing despite the numerous chats they had engaged in. She yearned to have an easy conversation, one free from awkward silences. They knew each other on a superficial basis, but the more they grew familiar with one another, the more the tedious pauses prevailed. Except there were no pauses when he found something to criticize about her person.

"The season is nearing its end," he said as she found her way back to his side.

Smile a serene smile and nod. Just as her former governess always instructed her to do when conversing with a gentleman. Maybe that tactic explained why her relationship with Lord Edwin felt so...stagnant. She could exert herself, show off some of her personality, and perchance they could engage in some enlivened chatter for a change.

"I cannot wait to return to the country so I can oversee my gardens."

Lord Edwin's brows drew together in a puzzled manner. "I had not realized you enjoyed gardening."

She tilted her head to the side. They never spoke about anything related to her hobbies. "I am particularly fond of roses."

Relief dawned in his dark blue eyes, and he smiled. "Roses are very feminine. I cannot say that I disapprove of your oversight of a rose garden."

"I do more than oversee, my lord." She sent him a parting smile as he handed her off to another partner.

When she returned to Lord Edwin he asked, "What do you do aside from supervising a few footmen?"

She chuckled at his misconception of her duties. The mere thought of burying her hands in some newly loosened, damp dirt brought a sense of happiness to her. "I do everything. I dig up the garden, plant new seeds, and remove the weeds."

She drifted to another gentleman but not before witnessing Lord Edwin's mouth slant down in an alarmingly dour frown. The dance dictated she pass to several other gentlemen before returning to Lord Edwin. As she glided to his side, she peered at him, and sure enough, his frown still lingered.

His hand grasped hers, and he pulled her to him. "I

cannot understand why you should engage in such menial tasks, my lady."

She shrugged. "I enjoy them."

"In the future, I shall guarantee you have enough servants that you will not need to suffer such plebian activities."

How could he believe gardening was plebian? She lived for gardening. Working the soil, seeing her hard work turn into beauty. Nothing would convince her to give up her passion. "I enjoy gardening, my lord. I want to continue doing what I enjoy."

"Do be realistic. You will not work in the garden like a common servant." He frowned, and she shuddered at the disapproval he exhibited.

The music tapered off, and she curtsied as he bowed. She cocked her head to the side and asked, "Do you not care for my happiness, my lord? You probably won't even notice my toils."

He softened and smiled as he led her off the dance floor. "Of course I do, my dear. I am sure we can come to a compromise at some point."

That was not what she wanted to hear, especially after his display of disapproval, but it would do for now. It wasn't as if he could keep her from the garden once they married. She nodded and dropped her gaze. Her attempt at furthering their acquaintance had failed, unless one considered resounding disapproval for her hobby a success. Yes, awkward silence would have been much better.

He left her at her mother's side, and Alexa went in search of Miss Cannis. Her slippers trod silently on the marble floors, and she unsurprisingly found Miss Cannis seated on the outskirts of the ballroom near the retiring room.

Alexa sank onto a chair next to Miss Cannis and asked, "How are you tonight?"

Miss Cannis sighed and focused on her hemline. Her wheat-colored curls shifted forward, and she shook her head. "It appears Lord Collins's very public snub has caused my one and only suitor to desert me."

Alexa pulled out her fan and swished it, her agitation evidenced by the force of her movement. She should have assumed Lord Collins had damaged Miss Cannis's reputation but had erred on the optimistic side. "How absurd that society would believe such rubbish. Lord Collins did not intend to snub you."

Or at least, he should not have intended to.

Miss Cannis shook her head and sent Alexa a scathing look. "And yet you defend him rather than comfort me. I thought you might act this way."

Alexa's sudden inhalation sounded pained even to her own ears. "You know I will side with you every time, especially in the face of such a ridiculous rumor."

"Ridiculous as it may be, it has happened." Her brown eyes narrowed on Alexa's, and Miss Cannis scowled. "Whispers of scandal seem to follow you. When I first met you, I thought you the sort to stay loyal through any storm. I never realized you were the one to cause the storms."

Dumbfounded, Alexa sat immobile, trapped both by the pain in her friend's eyes and the words she uttered. Miss Cannis stood and regarded Alexa with tears forming in her eyes. "I need time away from you to think. I have to do what is best for me, you know."

Miss Cannis turned on her heel and walked away. Her slippers barely made a sound, but each step sliced away at Alexa's heart. Alexa cringed as guilt encompassed her, and then she finally formed the words she wished she would have said. "I may cause the storms, but I also calm them."

Alexa couldn't fault Miss Cannis for the girl's anger, though. With her meager dowry and passable looks, Miss Cannis had struggled to find a match. Now that a peer of the realm had snubbed her, she would be hard-pressed to find anyone at all.

She rose from her chair and snatched a glass of champagne from a passing footman. She would fix this situation and repair the damage to her friend, no matter what. She took a sip of the bubbly liquid and scowled. If only Lord Collins had deigned to make an appearance tonight, but of course he had to be difficult. She could not very well search for him now, but she could arrange to meet him in the morning.

The earlier the better. And then, later in the day, she would nap.

Chapter 4

The morning was much too warm for Maxon's liking, although truth be told, most mornings were dreadful after a serious night of carousing. His head pounded, but he could not ignore the note that had been sent up that morning.

Alexa needed to see him about a shameful, delicate matter. That was all her alarming note had said. When he first read the missive, he had not known what to think, but the more he pondered the options, the more his mind jumped to all sorts of terrifying things that might have befallen her. Namely, that that damnable Lord Edwin had done something unsavory to her.

Coffee had been sent up, and the butler had looked alarmed to see his expression. His valet, Chaney, had already managed to dress him in proper riding clothes, but Maxon had barely registered the clothing on his body.

All he wanted was to strangle Lord Edwin.

The only reason he had not rushed over to challenge Lord Edwin to a duel was because he needed to hear the truth from Alexa first. That, and he needed to ensure she had actually been compromised. He held onto a smidgen of hope, but his gut told him he was right to assume the worst.

He swiftly downed his coffee and headed out the door.

His dark bay stallion, Tyr, stood saddled and waiting for him. The saddle creaked as he mounted, and he whispered soothingly to his horse. The time had just struck nine o'clock, which meant he would be early for this meeting. He rode on anyway and stopped right outside of the entrance to Hyde Park.

The wind was strong that morning but not strong enough to stave off the heat of summer. That dreadful temperature did not make his head feel any better, nor did it keep people from the outdoors. The park was filling up with those desirous of taking the air, and plenty of people made sure to greet him on the way in.

Several minutes passed, and he grew more irritated by each jovial welcome and angrier at Alexa for her stupidity. Until he spotted her with her groom trailing a short distance behind.

Her dark blue riding habit hugged her curves, and he couldn't help but notice the way she moved atop her horse. Despite his headache, a strong yearning overtook him to take the place of her mount. The way she rode elicited sinful thoughts of her above him with soft, satin sheets intertwined amongst their limbs.

His headache was forgotten as Alexa smoothed her unruly hair back. He grinned at the thought of her propensity for messiness. Even now, she rearranged her tangled skirts. How she managed to tangle them was beyond him, seeing as she rode sidesaddle and her skirts should never have had an opportunity to move in the first place.

The whinny of a horse brought her attention from her skirts to the source of the sound, and she straightened when her eyes met his. She self-consciously tucked a piece of hair away, and Maxon's anger returned. How could she succumb to Lord Edwin of all people?

He glowered as she reached his side. "Good morning, my lady. You should be grateful I waited until the designated time to meet with you. I had half a mind to rush over immediately upon receiving your note."

Alexa waved her hand and gave him a chilling smile. "Do not be absurd. The specified time in my note was early enough."

"Early enough?" Her reaction was not at all what he expected. "What has the bastard done?"

Alexa raised her eyebrow. "Please lighten your tone, my lord, otherwise people will talk." She guided her horse through the gates of Hyde Park, not bothering to check if he followed or not.

Had the woman gone mad? Why would she behave in such an unconcerned fashion? He caught up to her and offered a fake smile he was certain resembled more of a grimace. His teeth were tightly clenched as he asked, "Well? What is the problem? Have you been compromised?"

Her mouth fell open, exposing a set of white, even teeth. "Why on earth would you think I had been compromised?"

"You said you had to speak with me on a shameful, delicate matter." His scowl deepened at the thought of her at the mercy of Lord Edwin. A chill crept up his spine as he realized another possibility. Could the delicate matter mean she was *enceinte*?

She nodded at a passing couple, and he inspected her abdomen. It looked as flat as ever, yet it could be too soon for her to show. Should she ride a horse if she were increasing?

"Ahem." She coughed, and he tore his gaze from her waistline. Tall trees surrounded them, and luckily, all neighboring people were out of hearing.

"I assume Lord Edwin is the father?" he asked, trying his best to rein in his temper.

"The father?" Her brows drew together in confusion and she said, "This really has nothing to do with Lord Edwin."

He was not yet thirty, yet he swore he would have a heart attack. "Who, then?"

"Why, Miss Cannis, of course."

He was trying his best to follow her train of thought, but he was at a loss. "Miss Cannis is *enceinte*?"

Her brows furrowed even more at his question. "Of course not. Who told you that?"

If Alexa had not been compromised and neither girl was pregnant, then what was this all about? "So, why are we here?"

"To speak of your damage to Miss Cannis's reputation, of course."

"Of course?" He almost shouted the words. He had been in a state of worry all morning, which had increased tenfold when he thought she might be pregnant. Despite his agitation with her, relief washed over him that no one had been compromised.

Gavin would bloody well murder him if she had been ruined his first week on the job.

Despite his relief, his headache returned, and he rubbed his temple. She was aggravating, to put it mildly. "I did not retire until early morning. I barely slept a wink before I received your note. Now you tell me I came here for some unimportant reason? Why

41

couldn't this have waited until later?"

A cloud passed over the sun, and his headache abated marginally with the absence of the bright rays.

"I have calls to make later."

Of course she did.

She waved her hand. "Besides, my reason to meet with you is hardly unimportant."

"Oh? How is it not?" He turned and nodded at a passing acquaintance. They were on one of the main paths, but it was not yet the social time in Hyde Park, and the farther they delved into the park, the fewer people they would meet.

"If you do not fix what you have done to her, she will be ruined."

His horse threw its head and neighed loudly, and Maxon leaned over to calm him. He straightened and shook his head. "She is not ruined. Stop being overly dramatic."

Her eyes flashed, and she tilted her head. For a brief moment, he thought her hat might fall off, but it remained precariously in place. "It is hardly dramatic. You have a knack for ruining people, intentionally or not."

"Are you still holding on to your grudge against me? I apologized the other night."

"Of course I hold a grudge. If Lady Laura had not stepped in—"

He cut her off before she could finish the sentence. "Then I would have married you and saved your reputation." He looked at her, allowing his anger to shine through with that glare. "How little you must think of me if you imagined I would sit idly by and watch you face social ruin, especially when it *was* partially my fault."

She stared into his eyes and her lips parted.

Those lips. All pouty and inviting.

What the deuce? His errant thoughts needed to end. Now.

She appeared oblivious to his inner turmoil as she whispered, "I apologize, my lord. I had not realized you would behave so selflessly."

Her soft statement helped. She had impugned his honor by thinking so little of him, after all. He cleared his throat. "Well, now you do."

Her words made him uncomfortable, more uncomfortable than thinking of kissing those cherry lips. Even if she had been a gargoyle, he had a strong sense of honor and would have done the right thing. Especially when it came to his best friend's little sister. Granted, the way she looked now, it would not have been a selfless act at all.

A passing lady on horseback pulled to a halt next to Alexa, and Alexa cheerily chatted with her. Maxon allowed them to converse for a few moments and then coughed. He raised an eyebrow and asked Alexa, "Shall we, my lady?"

Alexa addressed the lady once more, and the two laughed. She waved goodbye and then returned her attention to Maxon, who was waiting as patiently as he could. "I suggest we keep moving, otherwise we will be forced into talking with every nosy passerby."

"I should think you would welcome people's approaches so you could snub those you find beneath you."

He raised his brow and met her eyes with his. A reply would only gratify her, so he turned his attention to the front and kicked Tyr into a trot. Never in his life had he tried to openly snub a lady on purpose, unless she deserved it. A gentleman, well, that was different. Some gentlemen were just too much to bother with.

The leaves on the trees rustled with the wind, and the tall grass along the path swayed. A rider approached, and as he neared, Maxon made out the rather large form of Lord Edwin. A bad taste filled his mouth at the sight of the man. This day could not get any more aggravating.

Suspicion clouded Lord Edwin's eyes as he looked at Maxon and pulled up on his reins. He turned his frown to Alexa and asked, "Who is this, my lady?"

His tone did not seem to faze her and she said sweetly, "Lord Edwin, this is Lord Collins. My brother has appointed him to act as a chaperone of sorts for the rest of the season."

"Oh."

Maxon tensed when Lord Edwin did not turn to greet him. The gentleman was clearly disconcerted that his lady rode with another gentleman, but he should not openly snub an earl.

"Who told you to pair that hat with that dress, my lady?" Lord Edwin asked, his eyes skimming over her in critical disdain.

Maxon inspected Alexa's hat and failed to see what Lord Edwin referred to. Her habit was dark blue, and the hat was cream with blue flowers on it. Maybe Edwin had switched from bullying classmates to bullying unwed misses.

"They match, my lord," Alexa stated without betraying any emotion.

"No. The shades of blue do not work."

The tension inside of Maxon increased with each word Lord Edwin uttered. He did not care if her clothes were not quite right, or that she had agitated him endlessly this morning. Or, for that matter, that she tended to irritate him every time he saw her. No one talked to Alexa that way. "Do you care for a bout of fisticuffs, Lord Edwin? You must if you so easily disparage Miss Farris in my presence."

Lord Edwin gave Maxon a haughty sneer and sat up straighter. "Who did you say you are? You obviously have no grasp of fashion."

Maxon smiled. The bloke must not remember him. "Earls do not need a grasp on fashion. If I spread word that Miss Farris dressed impeccably today, every lady in London will adopt the same style tomorrow."

The ice in his voice would freeze the most hot-blooded gentleman, and evidently, it worked on Lord Edwin as well. The color drained from Lord Edwin's face while anger entered his eyes.

Maxon turned to Alexa and asked, "Does he belittle you often?"

She swallowed. "He gives his opinion sometimes—"

"Which means you have taken far too many liberties, Lord Edwin. You will not do so again."

Lord Edwin snorted. "What goes on between Miss Farris and me is none of your concern."

"It most certainly is." His voice was steel, and he inhaled to calm himself.

"She needs a certain amount of guidance. Surely, you understand that."

Lord Edwin looked as though he believed what he said. Naturally, Maxon did not agree, and he walked his stallion closer to Lord Edwin until he was seated next to the gentleman. Maxon leaned in and whispered with a sneer, "I suggest you run along. I have been desirous of hitting something today, and you will do better than most."

"I will not leave." He huffed, and some of the color returned to his face. "I am not afraid of you."

"You should be."

A squirrel darted out from the trees, and Alexa's horse reared from the surprise. She neatly managed to keep her seat, all while keeping her hat in place. Maxon witnessed it from his peripheral, but the scene was over before he could do anything. He glanced back to Lord Edwin, and was dismayed to find Lord Edwin's attention still planted on him.

"Are you all right, my lady?" Maxon asked as he turned back to her.

Alexa smoothed her hair. "Of course." She smiled at Lord Edwin and asked, "Can we discuss this later? I would like to continue my ride."

Lord Edwin huffed and turned his horse to go around the pair. "Of course," he muttered in passing. He then shot a dark glare at Maxon and continued down the path.

Horse hooves beat against the dirt trail, decreasing in volume with each passing moment. Maxon attempted to rein in his temper. The one thing that could aggravate him most was someone treating Alexa poorly. Yes, she bothered him in a way that made him want to bend her over and give her a good spanking, but *he* would be the one to administer such punishment. No one else.

Finally, when his thoughts cleared, he looked at her. Her deep blue eyes appeared larger than usual, and they were filled with a gravity he had never witnessed before. Those eyes were something he would not soon forget, and in that moment, he decided that he would never allow her to marry Lord Edwin. Of course, Maxon could not simply tell her not to marry the bloke. He had to make her believe she made the decision on her own.

"So, you have met him. What do you think?" Her laugh sounded hollow.

"I think you can do much better." His voice held conviction unlike his normal aloofness, but he needed her to feel her own worth.

She stopped her horse as she bristled, and he was forced to stop Tyr as well. Her mare sidestepped, and Alexa calmed her. "He is almost without compare. Why, many ladies dream of snaring Lord Edwin."

"He seems a bit too critical."

"He is the very epitome of a gentleman. He might be critical, but that is only because he is in the highest state of fashion."

Maxon was not convinced in the slightest. "So, he's a dandy."

"No."

"Uh-huh." He chuckled his disbelief. She speared him with a dark look and spurred her mare on.

He caught up with ease and almost laughed at the rebellious expression on her face. All mirth receded when her look turned to one of outright fury.

"You have done wrong here, my lord, and you must repair the damage you have done."

The trail narrowed, so Maxon allowed Alexa to ride first. He followed her and could have sworn he caught a scent of roses. The curves of her waistline momentarily distracted him until she interrupted his trance. "You might act indifferent to Miss Cannis's plight, but *you* caused her broken heart. How can you not feel even a smidgen of remorse?"

"What broken heart?"

"The one you inflicted upon her! She had a suitor, but because of your rudeness, now has none."

The words sank in, and Maxon's heart constricted. He liked to believe his chest contained nothing but the shriveled remnants of the heart he used to have, but secretly, he knew better. "If the gentleman is willing to cut ties with her so easily, then I did her a favor."

"Miss Ashford cut ties with you just as easily, yet where did that leave you?" Maxon's eyes narrowed on her, but she ignored him. "And when Miss Cannis's gentleman weds as quickly as Miss Ashford did, or should I say Her Grace, do you suppose that will somehow lessen her distress?"

Her eyes held his, conveying her message in a way words could not. He had not tried to snub Miss Cannis. Rather, Alexa's situation had blinded him to Miss Cannis's existence altogether. Seeing Alexa and discovering a new attraction for her had destroyed all the good manners he would typically employ.

He kept his overall mien unreadable, but inside, remorse for his callous actions built. "What do you suggest I do to remedy my error?"

"Escort her somewhere. Make sure all of society sees you with her and understands you do not believe her to be bad *ton*."

He processed her words as another cloud passed over the sun. He broke eye contact and regarded the sky. Many more clouds dotted the sky than when he first emerged out of doors. He would have felt relief over the sun's absence, but couldn't. Not now.

Finally, he brought his eyes back to hers, and he tensed at the frustration he read there. "Fair enough, but in the future, arrange for meetings later in the day."

They rode in uncomfortable silence for a short while, and then she looked around surreptitiously before she, once again, rearranged her skirts. He was forced to smile, until her hat finally toppled over. She gasped as her hand flew to intercept the hat, but it fell to the ground with a thud.

He dismounted and picked it up. It was remarkably heavy. "Do all ladies wear such burdensome hats?"

The corners of her lips twitched, and she snatched the hat from him as he handed it to her. Her adept fingers straightened the crooked stems until they appeared normal once more. "Mother was convinced it needed more flowers." She placed it back on her head and stuck her hat pin back in place.

"What are the flowers made of? Lead?" His hand rested on the neck of the horse, far enough from her person for propriety's sake but close enough to make him too aware of her. He itched to slide his hand over to that tantalizing leg, no matter how inadvisable.

This time, she did smile down at him, and his pulse accelerated. "I am not sure, but Mother delighted in the outcome. I must admit it weighs more than my other ones."

"I am sure it does." His hand fell away from temptation, and he returned to Tyr. After mounting, he nodded, and they continued their ride.

He pulled at his collar. It was so bloody hot out here, and it would only worsen as the day wore on.

All because of her.

They rounded a bend in the tree-lined trail, and Alexa covered her mouth to stifle a yawn. "I wish we could have done this later in the day. I am so very tired."

Of all the…He caught himself before he started swearing. "I wish we could have avoided this altogether."

She scowled at him. "You do not understand the sacrifice I made this morning. Normally, I do not rise this early."

As if he would thank her for her alarming note. He glowered at her.

She ignored his look, her expression turning quite winsome as she nodded and waved at a passerby. They must be nearing the entrance to Hyde Park, as evidenced by the increase in riders. The sun played off her exposed hair, and he was struck by the colors displayed there. Her brown tresses held a cooler tone but aside from that, the color was eerily similar to his horse's coat.

He chuckled, and she turned to regard him. "Is something amusing, my lord?"

He coughed. "I just had the most unusual realization."

"Oh?" She smiled, but it was a reserved smile as if she knew she would not like what he said. "Do you care to share your epiphany?"

"Yes, as a matter of fact, it relates to you and my comely steed." He patted Tyr and smiled. She would not appreciate the comparison, but he would enjoy her reaction immensely.

Her expression turned wary. "Enlighten me. How

do I relate to your horse?"

"You asked, so it is not my fault if you are angry. Tyr's coat is almost the exact same color as your hair."

She masked her look of surprise and turned to peruse his horse with a skeptical tilt to her eyebrow. "No. You are wrong, my lord."

"I do not believe I am."

"Of course you are."

He laughed. She always had been able to amuse him. "No, but you can disprove my notion. Come over here and place your head next to my mount."

She shuddered. "I will not, and even if I did, you would probably lie and claim we match."

His already present grin broadened. "Well then, give me a lock of your hair."

"I will not!" she said, straightening as if slapped. "Only lovers give each other such a personal keepsake."

He tensed as she said the word *lovers*. His previous image of them in bed together returned, and his gaze settled on her lips. There was no possible reason for him to consider her disrobed, yet he could not stop himself. "Well, we needn't tell anyone, but if you insist you will not, then that means I am right by default."

She straightened in her saddle. "You, my lord, are a cad."

He shrugged the comment aside. "Now why would you say that? I personally like your hair color."

"I would have thought you preferred blonds."

He had preferred blonds. After all, Miss Ashford was blond, but recently, he had begun to appreciate darker colorings. "Now you know better, my lady."

She remained silent and he eyed her. "What about

51

you? Do you prefer brunettes like Lord Edwin?" He was not sure why he asked, but now he eagerly awaited her response.

She dipped her head as a rosy blush stained her cheeks. "I am uncertain."

He grinned. She was a joy to tease. "I know you have a preference. Come now, you can tell me."

She patted her mare, keeping her eyes averted, and whispered, "I suppose the color of your hair is pleasant."

His breath caught. Could Alexa find him attractive? He nixed that thought before it could take hold. He would have noticed at the start of the season if she felt anything stronger than friendship for him.

Yes, he would have noticed. How could he not, when she had compelled him to look at her every chance he received? He appreciated all women, though, so he oughtn't feel guilty.

Except for when his thoughts turned to bedchamber activities. Then, he should feel downright ashamed.

She regarded him with a shuttered expression, and he shook himself. "Yes, well, we shall simply replace Lord Edwin with a blond gentleman, then."

Something flashed across her eyes, something uncomfortably like pain. "Absolutely, my lord. Should I end things with Lord Edwin, we can indeed find a blond gentleman. I am sure one will do as well as any other, so it will be simple."

"Those are rather strange sentiments for a lady to have. What happened to love?"

She did not return her gaze to his and instead focused on the point between her mare's ears. "If I cannot wed my beloved, then I suppose any other gentleman will do."

"I hadn't realized you were that devoted to him."
He hated to destroy a love match, but Lord Edwin was
unacceptable. Better she experience a broken heart than
a lifetime with someone unworthy.

She shrugged and didn't say anything.

They rode in silence, and Maxon wracked his brain
with ways to cheer her. Now that he had learned to
appreciate her lips, he would prefer to see them
displayed in a smile. She clearly loved Lord Edwin, but
their marriage was not meant to be.

He could find a blond worthy of her and hope they
fell in love, but each gentleman he thought of seemed
wrong. She might just have to live with heartbreak and
find a new suitor on her own in the future.

That was the only option.

The entrance to Hyde Park loomed before them,
and he broke the stillness. "You may not believe me
now, but someday you will find someone even better
than him. Someone that is deserving of your devotion,
and then you will thank me for saving you from this
disastrous union."

Her grim smile tugged at his conscience, but he
would take any smile she offered over her frown. "I am
sure you are correct, my lord. After all, you have
recovered so successfully from your own heartbreak."

He ignored her sarcasm as the sadness in her voice
pierced his heart. He opened his mouth to say
something, but she turned her head away, blocking the
sorrow in her eyes, and spurring her mare toward the
entrance. He would allow her to leave unimpeded, and
someday she would see reason.

A heavy guilt lay on his shoulders, which increased

as she rode away. Her groom trailed behind her, just as he had throughout their ride, and Maxon had to crane his neck to continue watching her. Luckily, he caught himself before anyone noticed his obvious interest in her.

Her curves really were distracting, and he should never have noticed them in the first place. He was a cad, just as she said.

Chapter 5

The warm, humid night air signified summer was upon them. Maxon's stuffy cravat and evening jacket did little to repel the stifling heat, and he wished for the hundredth time that he was to attend the theater tonight, or any other gathering rather than Vauxhall Gardens. Unfortunately, he had promised to make amends to Alexa's friend, and if that meant venturing out in the muggy night air, then so be it.

He pulled out his watch and scowled as he realized he was late. Granted, he only had to search the tables to find his party, so he was not *that* late. He scanned the crowd for Alexa and cursed at how busy the gardens were. This place was too large for him to scrutinize on his own, but there were no other options. So, he searched.

Finally, he spotted a familiar pile of curly brown hair turned in conversation with a gentleman. His eyes narrowed as he recognized Lord Edwin, and an unusual tide of anger hit him at how closely the two were seated. Lord Edwin should not enjoy such a position. No, Lord Edwin deserved the companionship of the conniving sort. Namely any other lady than Alexa.

He thrust aside his feelings and approached the party with a smile.

"You are here. Finally." Alexa's greeting was cool without so much as a how-do-you-do. She left a gloved hand on Lord Edwin's forearm, which Maxon chose to ignore.

"Of course, Miss Farris." He swept a glance over Lord Edwin and laced his words with derision. "I see our party is a bit larger than I expected."

She smiled in response. "I cannot answer to what you expected, my lord." She shifted closer to Lord Edwin. "I believe you have already met Lord Edwin."

He gave a sharp nod and turned to greet Lady Farris, who introduced him to Mrs. Cannis. Then, he approached Miss Cannis and bowed gallantly over her hand, placing a chaste kiss on the back of it. "It is a pleasure to see you again, my lady."

Miss Cannis blushed a fiery shade of red and drew her hand back as she managed to stutter an appropriate reply. Maxon claimed an empty seat next to Miss Cannis, which also happened to occupy the space across from Alexa, and did his best to not look in Alexa's direction.

His attempt to avoid her was futile, though. Alexa looked glorious tonight. Glorious enough to make him look twice, and then a third time for good measure. Her hair rebelled against its confines, and she wore a frothy creation in light blue which was delectable. And much too low-cut.

Maxon settled into his chair, trying to keep himself from looking at Alexa. Lord Edwin leaned forward and said, "I don't know why I didn't remember you. We met long ago at school, did we not?"

Maxon grunted an affirmation and poured himself some tea. Spirits were available here, and he would order a brandy as soon as the opportunity arose. He settled his attention on his tea and spooned a bit of sugar into his cup. He didn't always use sugar, but tonight it seemed a necessary indulgence. Especially when Alexa whispered something to Lord Edwin. He continued to add sugar to his cup as he glanced up to observe Alexa flirting unabashedly with Lord Edwin. She hung on Lord Edwin rather shamelessly, and it turned Maxon's stomach.

Miss Cannis interrupted his thoughts. "My lord, are you sure you desire that much sugar?"

"Of course." He stirred his tea and took a sip. He came close to gagging at how astronomically sweet the beverage was. The tea could not have been more undrinkable, but he smiled at Miss Cannis as if everything was perfect. "This is just how I take my tea."

She looked unsure as she muttered, "Of course, my lord."

The matter was settled, and he swung his gaze back to Alexa, who still conversed with Lord Edwin, or rather, listened politely as he spoke. She sat at a perfect position to allow Lord Edwin to peer down upon her décolletage, and Lord Edwin had left his eyes there for much too long. Maxon clenched his hands to hold himself back from reaching across the table to drag Lord Edwin away.

Suddenly, Alexa swung her gaze to his. She had caught him staring and appeared unfazed by it. "My lord, we thought to take a stroll. Would you care to accompany us?"

He was not about to allow Alexa to walk in the gardens alone with Lord Edwin, so he agreed. "Only if Miss Cannis would do me the honor of accompanying me." Alexa's eyes narrowed, and he gave her a ghost of a smile in return.

"Of course," Miss Cannis agreed, her cheeks tinging pink.

"If you don't mind, Mrs. Cannis and I will stay at the table," Lady Farris said with a smile.

Everyone agreed, and Lord Edwin guided Alexa toward one of the paths. Maxon, naturally, followed on their heels with Miss Cannis on his arm. Lanterns hung on either side of them to light their way, while tall green bushes surrounded them and seemed to transport them to another world, one where hordes of people were not within earshot.

He would not allow Alexa to leave his sight, as any proper brother's best friend would do. Never mind his unusual penchant for scandalous thoughts about the lady. Those were best ignored.

Lord Edwin led the party on a more secluded path, and Maxon congratulated himself once more. Far less attractive ladies than Alexa had been compromised in Vauxhall Gardens, despite the number of lanterns set along the path for light. Given the chance, Lord Edwin would undoubtedly avail himself of the opportunity to compromise Alexa out here. After all, the elegant line of her neck looked enticingly seductive in the moonlight. Her skin shone unblemished in the meager lighting and practically begged for fairy-light kisses to grace its exposed canvas.

He tore his gaze away as bits of the couple's conversation drifted back to him. Lord Edwin was audible despite his obvious attempt at secrecy. "How unfortunate you had to bring them along tonight. I had hoped for some time alone with you."

She murmured something unintelligible in

response, which caused Lord Edwin to smile and nod.

A strange tightening overtook his stomach at the sight of them. Whatever the feeling was, he did not like it, so instead, he allowed his eyes to skim over her voluminous hair, down her femininely curved back, and ending at her delectable derriere. It galled him that she would choose Lord Edwin to bestow such beauty upon, yet she did.

Again, he forced himself to look away from her figure and instead surveyed the path. Vines intertwined in the bushes, and flowering plants aided the gardens in their pleasant aroma. He strove to remain entertained by the foliage but couldn't seem to avoid glancing at Alexa. The way she walked enchanted him, especially in the candlelight where the shadows gave a vision of shifting allure.

They followed along the secluded pathway as Maxon searched for reasons to tear the two apart, when suddenly, Alexa stumbled. Lord Edwin caught her, but in his haste to steady her, his hand skimmed her bosom. Maxon's brows rose skyward in disbelief. No gentleman should take such liberties, especially in plain view of others.

He waited for her to slap Lord Edwin or do something to deter such behavior but nothing happened. They simply resumed walking.

"Miss Farris," Maxon said in a tight, angry voice. "Might I have a word?"

Alexa turned and gave him a curious look. "Of course, my lord." She released her escort's arm and walked carefully to Maxon, who then led her out of hearing from the others.

"You must take him to task for such an insult." He

scowled. Imagine how deplorably Lord Edwin might act if left alone with her?

Alexa's eyes widened, and Maxon recognized the anger building in those steely thunder-tinged orbs. "Excuse me? What is it you accuse him of?"

"Why…" He swallowed. Saying these words was not easy. "His hand and your bosom…" His voice trailed off as her eyes widened.

"Are you suggesting he did something improper?"

Her eyes were turning that grayish-blue which entranced him. Of course, the tint of her eyes did not bode well for how she reacted to their conversation. "Yes." He held up a hand to stop her angry retort and said, "I am not saying you allowed him, but you have not married him yet and should not allow such a crude act to pass without raising issue."

She hissed her response, which incrementally grew louder. "I don't know what you think you saw, but he did not touch me, except to steady me."

"His hand overreached if his sole aim was to steady you."

"Why, I never!" She huffed and thrust her hands on her hips. "What does it matter to you? My relationship with him is none of your business."

"Yes, it is."

"No, it is not."

Lord Edwin called over to them, "Is everything all right over there? I thought I heard a quarrel."

Alexa did not even look at Lord Edwin as she said, "All is well." Her eyes blazed, and she leaned in toward Maxon, which granted him an appreciable viewpoint of her bosom. She inhaled sharply. "Eyes up here, please."

He tore his gaze from the scintillating mounds and

raised an eyebrow. "Yes?" Why could she not have corrected Lord Edwin when he had stared at her for a seemingly endless span of time?

"I must return to my escort, but this is *not* over." She broke eye contact and returned to Lord Edwin's side. She whispered something to Lord Edwin, and then they resumed their stroll down the path, both appearing relaxed and appreciative of the night.

Maxon wanted to curse as he returned to Miss Cannis's side. He was not sure what he had hoped to accomplish, but he had failed whatever it was. He tugged at his starched collar. This path was devoid of a breeze and was insufferably hot.

"You dislike him."

Miss Cannis's astute observation surprised Maxon. "Am I so obvious in my distrust of the bloke?"

She shrugged and said in a meek voice, "I am not overly fond of him either."

"Yes, well, I cannot understand what she sees in him." He growled those words and, judging by the startled look in Miss Cannis's eyes, had shocked her.

She swallowed and asked, "Aside from his good looks and wealth, you mean?"

"Surely that cannot be all she requires in a match?" Maxon asked in disbelief.

"Plenty of members of the *ton* consider him to be quite the catch."

"That may be," he acknowledged, "but he is not without his flaws."

Miss Cannis nodded her head, and the soft glow of the lanterns enhanced her already large eyes. "But when has Miss Farris been the sort to listen to reason?"

Maxon could not agree with that statement more.

Alexa had always been hard-headed, and once her mind was made up, there was no changing it.

"So…" He coughed. He hated the fact that he was about to initiate gossip. "What are some of his flaws?"

Miss Cannis gave him a secretive smile and began regaling him of all the things she had heard about Lord Edwin. Not that there were many negative aspects to the man, but what she had was straight from Alexa's mouth, which was pure gold.

Maxon's lips slowly turned up in a cunning grin. He could use every last bit of information Miss Cannis provided him. When she finished, he swept a small bow. "I am forever in your debt, and if you are ever in need of my assistance, just ask."

Chapter 6

Lord Collins's eyes bore into Alexa's back for the entirety of their walk. Naturally, she did her best to act enamored with Lord Edwin to prove her claim of love, and it seemed to have worked. But then, her plan had also backfired. Lord Edwin behaved more and more familiarly with her as the night progressed, but she could not end the charade now.

Her ride with Lord Collins had been disastrous, aside from accomplishing what she set out to do. Much of her anger had receded when he claimed he would have married her to save her reputation, not that she would ever have allowed him to sacrifice himself in such a manner.

But his offer pulled at her heart.

And she did not need her heart to grow attached. Indeed, if she could convince herself to hate him, life would be much simpler.

Who could hate Lord Collins, though? Looks aside, he was a witty and humorous gentleman, although their chat about hair colors would have been best avoided. She could not help but blush at how she told Lord Collins she preferred gentlemen with his coloring. He had not deserved such an indirect compliment. It was beyond mortifying, seeing as he considered her on the same level as his horse. Her inability to think thoughts through before speaking was not beneficial, and she had best learn to rein in her tongue.

"Now then, Miss Farris, wouldn't you agree this night is almost approaching perfection?" Lord Edwin's gaze flicked to her hair, and she swept a dark strand behind her ear.

She forced herself to smile and nod, despite his use of that damned word again. Oh, dear. It would appear her irritation toward that word had grown to the point of employing foul language. That was *not* a good sign.

He acknowledged the reparation she made with a nod. "I would imagine the food will have arrived by the time we return to our table. I know my dear father would accept no less, and neither shall I. Not if our night is to be perfection personified."

"Of course," Alexa agreed and attempted to refrain from sighing. He had managed to bring up his father twice so far tonight, and once right before his favorite word. Alexa steered the topic of conversation down a different path. "I understand you are to depart for the country soon, my lord."

"Yes, but not for another month. My estate requires some attention, you know."

"Where is your estate located?"

His hand lingered on the small of her back as they rounded a bend in the path. The air had begun to cool, but it was warm enough to cause Alexa to perspire. Unfortunately, she had left her fan at the table, so she would just have to survive the stifling heat.

"It is located right down the road from Father's main estate, Nettleridge. He bought it just for me."

"How thoughtful of him." He nodded, and she continued, "Is it a large estate?" His hand was still on her back, so she broke away from him under the pretense of inspecting a flower.

Lord Maxon and Miss Cannis stopped to wait, and Alexa couldn't help but look twice at the pair. The pair deep in conversation. What could they have to speak of that required such intensity?

"Come away, my dear. We must return to our party."

Alexa took his arm and allowed her stiff posture to relax infinitesimally when he did not place his hand on her back once more. While she did not mind touching him, she did not prefer intimate touches from him. No matter how slight.

He smiled at her and patted his face with a handkerchief. "In answer to your question, yes, it is a large estate. My father was exceedingly gracious."

She could understand speaking of his father in such a context as this. It was just when Lord Edwin spoke of him as if his opinion held more merit than the king's that she grew annoyed. "I should like to see your estate someday, my lord. Is there a pond or other body of water? I do love to enjoy nature while reading."

He frowned. "Do you read often?"

"Sometimes."

His frown intensified. "I cannot say I condone such bluestocking tendencies."

She shrugged. "I am sorry to hear you say that, my lord."

He considered her for a moment and said, "I suppose I can allow it if you promise to do it at home, and out of the public eye."

"How thoughtful." How had it taken this long for his hatred of reading to come up in conversation? It seemed the closer they came to marriage, the more he showed his real colors.

He clasped her hand in his and brought it to his lips as they walked, which was rather awkward. "You know, I do try to be thoughtful. That is one thing you can count on in our marriage."

She smiled as if impressed. The line of bushes looked as though they ended up ahead, and Alexa could almost feel the breeze that would greet her when they exited from the path.

Sure enough, the end was at hand, and Alexa was spared further conversation as Lord Edwin guided her to her seat.

"The food has all been served!" Alexa's mother exclaimed as everyone sat down.

As Alexa moved to sit, she sneaked a peek at Lord Collins across the table and was dismayed to find him staring back at her with an annoyingly smug look on his too-charming face. She dropped her gaze to her plate and proceeded to cut her paper-thin slices of ham into tiny pieces.

Lord Collins's deep voice penetrated the silence. "Lord Edwin, a lot of time has passed since Eton, has it not?"

Lord Edwin chuckled. "Ah yes, the good old days." He took a bite of his food and looked quizzically at Lord Collins. "We were not in the same year, correct?"

Alexa ceased cutting her ham when Lord Edwin replied. She looked up at the sound of his voice but, upon seeing the food in his mouth, returned with renewed vigor to cutting her meat. How could such a particular man have such lax manners? He never made even the slightest attempt to curtail his rude behavior, either.

"I am afraid not, although I was only a couple years behind you."

"Yes, well, Father always says the only school worth attending is Eton, and Cambridge, of course."

"Of course," Lord Collins said, even though Alexa knew full well he had not attended Cambridge. He had attended Oxford, just as Gavin had. "How is your father, anyway? He did not make it to town for the season, did he?"

"Whilst that would have suited me perfectly, he does not like to come to town. I, myself, would not be here if I were not in need of a wife."

"Your father is not married? Does he intend to stay a bachelor?"

Lord Edwin smiled and shook his head. He bit into his ham once more and said, "No. Father thinks it best he remains unwed. He believes he is too old to take a wife, but I disagree. Any young lady would love to marry him and would consider it an honor."

Alexa picked up her own glass of wine and took a sip. Lord Edwin could speak endlessly about his father, if given the chance. She glanced about the table until she settled on Miss Cannis. Miss Cannis looked guilty, but Alexa hadn't the faintest idea why.

Lord Edwin finished chewing his last bite, and Alexa's irritation eased. She wouldn't have to watch him speak with his mouth full any longer. At least, not until Lord Collins took note of Lord Edwin's empty plate. "Would you care for more ham?"

"You know, I don't mind if I do." He secured several slices from the tray in the center of the table and took a bite. Alexa nearly groaned out loud as he said, "Father deserves to marry again, but he made me promise to find myself a wife before he even countenances the notion."

Lord Collins lifted his glass of wine and asked over the brim, "Oh, and have you found her?"

"I think so. She is almost perfect, you know."

"But will your father approve? I can't imagine you would marry without his approval." Lord Collins took a drink of his wine, betraying not a shred of emotion.

"Of course. My father has done so much for me, even as a second son. As a result, it is very important to me that he approve of my future bride."

Alexa's eyes widened as her head reared up. "You have already asked me to marry you. What would happen if I said yes, and then your father did not approve?"

Lord Edwin patted her hand. "He will."

"But if he doesn't?"

He chuckled, but he appeared excruciatingly uncomfortable at the situation. "He can't help but love you. I am positive he shall approve."

"What if you are wrong?"

"I am not wrong." His voice grew louder, chasing away some of his uncertainty with bravado.

Alexa's pulse slowed, and her palms grew damp. This was unbearable. "If he meets me, and dislikes me, you won't marry me?" Her question was more of a statement, and in her heart, she knew she was right. He didn't have to acknowledge her claim. She knew.

Lord Edwin's silence and averted gaze was answer enough. Lady Farris gasped, and Alexa's ears rang. It was completely unacceptable to break an engagement. Why, she would be ruined if he did that to her!

"We would never enter into a formal engagement

until my father approved."

Lord Collins surveyed him. His frigid look sent a shiver down Alexa's spine at its coolness while simultaneously sending a shiver of approval in the opposite direction. Lord Collins defended her. She nearly smiled as he said, "This plan of yours is unacceptable. Even a broken unofficial engagement would dictate pistols at dawn."

The blood drained from Lord Edwin's visage, and he turned to give Alexa a questioning look. She was unsure about Lord Collins's desire to duel Lord Edwin, but she quite agreed that Lord Edwin deserved a harsh penalty. "Luckily, there will be no need for a duel in defense of my honor. I have not entered into an engagement of any sort and will not do so under such conditions."

"What are you saying, Miss Farris?" Lord Edwin asked.

"I am saying, you will just have to wait to receive my response until I have met your father."

Lord Edwin nodded and exhaled his relief. He appeared unfazed by the general atmosphere at the table and responded with one simple word. "Perfect."

Except perfection did not describe a marriage to Lord Edwin. He had too many negative qualities. Amiss qualities. She ought to feel surprise at yet another, more grievous, mark against him, but she shockingly felt nothing. No remorse, no heartbreak, nothing.

Her attention returned to her ham. The formerly appetizing dish held no appeal, and not even the sight of the lush gardens around her could inspire her. She, the gardening enthusiast, found no pleasure in a garden. But how could she find pleasure when her evening had come to this? She had wasted five months on a courtship which might not come to fruition.

Lord Edwin should have determined her suitability *before* he offered for her hand.

When she looked up once more, Lord Collins nodded to her and rose. "I believe the night has reached its finale." He threw his linen napkin on the table and crossed to Alexa's side. "May I have the honor of a brief stroll with you, Miss Farris?"

She nodded and took his hand. To remain with Lord Edwin was far more taxing than a stroll with Lord Collins.

Her mother's chair squeaked as she moved to stand. "Give me a moment, and I shall chaperone you."

"Don't trouble yourself, my lady. We will remain in sight."

Lady Farris considered his words and then nodded. "Very well."

Lord Collins placed Alexa's hand in the crook of his arm and led her a short distance away. They were out of earshot of the table, next to a long row of bushes. A pleasant breeze wafted by to chase away the heat and also carried along the scent of mint.

His scent.

How strange she had never taken note of his smell before. Now, it would be etched into her memory for eternity.

"I am sorry he is such an idiot."

"Are you?" She swung to face him with a grim smile. He had made it abundantly clear he did not approve of Lord Edwin.

He sighed. His hand lingered on her elbow, absentmindedly playing with the excess fabric of her glove. "Not really. I am sorry for the pain he has caused you, but I am pleased nonetheless."

Pleased? But then, he would respond in such a manner. Even though Alexa held little emotional attachment to Lord Edwin, she still smarted from his harsh treatment of her. So *pleased* seemed a bit too callous, even for Lord Collins.

"Shall you break it off with him, then?"

She stepped away and pulled her arms around herself in a tight hold. His hand fell to his side, and his beautiful blue eyes clouded with concern. For her. Uncertainty held her within its torturous grasp. She should never speak to Lord Edwin again. This night should have determined her course of action, and yet Lord Collins would win. His duty would end, and he would leave.

"No," she said, her voice a shaky whisper.

"Why not?"

Why not, indeed? How to give an answer she did not know herself? Or rather, how could she give an answer she detested? She did not like her response to Lord Collins's proximity. If she could, she would have rid herself of her perpetual attraction for him ages ago. Her imperfect heart beat for a man who would never love her in return, yet she should send away a decent enough suitor?

Her laugh was bitter as she unwound her hands from her frame and stationed them at her side. She might choose to deny Lord Edwin's suit but not tonight. She couldn't bear to witness Lord Collins's gloating smile.

"He made a heedless mistake. He is hardly perfect," she said, her voice growing stronger, surer.

"Yes, but that mistake could have cost you your reputation."

She was in no mood to debate this with him, but she did so anyway. "Yes." She eyed him. "*If* I had agreed, and *if* his father disapproved, then yes, I would have been ruined."

"Which means you should listen to me and rid yourself of him now."

"Let me get this straight." She sneaked a furtive glance to ensure no one had drawn near and said in a low voice, "I should listen to you by cutting ties to Lord Edwin, and I should have hit him earlier when you claimed he made untoward contact with my person. Is there anything else I should be doing, my lord?"

"As a matter of fact—"

She cut him off before he could say anything further. "In case you are unaware, that was a rhetorical question. I don't wish to hear any more of the ways I have not met your standards."

He stepped to her, and she backed away. He scowled at her retreat, and he stopped his forward movement. "How is it you can behave so meekly toward him but give me a setdown at every opportunity?"

Her heartbeat quickened, and she clenched her hands. "That is the difference between how I treat people I like versus people I dislike."

His eyes narrowed and his voice quieted. "And now you dislike me?"

She swallowed. "Why should I not? Ever since you returned to London, you have done nothing but wreak havoc on my life."

The light breeze seemed to have forgotten them,

and she swore she could feel the flame from a lantern as it burned nearby. A cricket chirped in the background, and she shuddered as a sweat droplet trickled down her back.

His eyes appeared to darken as he shook his head and said, "I always treat you with the upmost respect. There is no reason for you to dislike me."

He may behave as he ought, but he was far from likable. He was downright, annoyingly, loveable. "So far, you have spoken negatively of Lord Edwin countless times. You show no consideration for my feelings, and you have never given me a single compliment."

"I have too given you compliments."

"Really?" She exhaled. "Name one."

He contemplated the matter for a moment and then said, "I told you your hair was prettier in disarray."

She had forgotten that. "So you said one thing. Congratulations."

"Thank you." He swept an exaggerated bow and smirked up at her.

"That is not something to be proud of. Why, it's not even that monumental a compliment."

He straightened, and a light flared in his eyes. There had always been a light mood between them, but he had never looked at her in such a way before. It was almost, well, sinful.

"Allow me to remedy my error, then." He caught her hand in his, and gazed deep into her eyes. "Your eyes remind me of a summer storm." Her gaze faltered from his, but he continued. "Your skin is as smooth as fine porcelain, and your hair is made of the most enticing curls I have ever seen. I can imagine your freed hair would make a man lose his senses. And lastly, you have deliciously kissable lips."

She swallowed. His ridiculous, probably oft-used lines had the most amazing effect on her. Her knees had grown weak, and her mind was slow to focus. "I-I d-don't think…" Her voice trailed off as he chuckled.

"With that said, you also possess a tremendous ability to irritate me beyond comprehension."

That shook her enough to end her weak-kneed response. She glared and straightened from her withered position. "You can't simply be pleasant, can you? You have to end on a sour note."

He shrugged. "If your behavior was not so irrational, I would not have needed to mention it."

"I have a logical explanation for my behavior."

"Which is?"

"I don't like you." Except she did. Too much.

The cricket chirped once more, interrupting the intensity of the moment with its grating music. "Honestly, darling, you do not need to like me. You just need to dislike Lord Edwin." His hand dropped hers, but not before he allowed it to slide down the length of her fingers.

Her stomach flipped pleasantly, and she brought her eyes up from his hand. He was so tall and equally as infuriating. She turned from him, her breath catching as she spoke. "We should return now."

"Of course."

She kept her hands clenched in front of her. She did not want to touch him. They strolled side by side and returned to the table, her attention rooted firmly to each step she took, rather than him.

"Is everything settled?" Lady Farris asked as Alexa

moved to sit.

"Yes, but where is Lord Edwin?" He was nowhere to be seen.

"He thought it best he leave so we could stay and enjoy the fireworks."

Odd how she had not noticed his departure. "Ah," Alexa murmured in response. While she preferred to avoid confronting him, it was exceptionally rude of him not to see her home, much less bid her good evening.

She looked up to find Lord Collins had resumed his position next to Miss Cannis. They chatted amiably, and Alexa remembered why they were there in the first place. "It is best we stay. Lord Collins still must repair the damage he has done."

"I am sure all is well." Alexa followed her mother's gaze to a passing group, and she identified Lady Chadwick in the throng, regally sporting her signature walking cane. Her aunt was a renowned gossip, and she had spotted them. Even now, she stalked to their table, her cane more for show than actual use.

"Alexa, my dear, are you here without male escort?" Lady Chadwick glanced around the table until she spotted Lord Collins. "Oh dear, I had heard rumors that you had returned and snubbed a young lady. What a dastardly thing to do." She giggled and sat down in Lord Edwin's former chair, propping her cane against the table and settling into the chair.

"It was not intentional, my lady." He gestured to Miss Cannis. "As you can see, I very much approve of her."

Her eyes sharpened on Miss Cannis. "I see. Those gossips are always getting things wrong." Never mind that she was one of the biggest gossips.

She turned to her friends and motioned them to continue on their way. "I think I will spend the rest of the evening with my family." Lady Chadwick waited for her party to depart then asked, "Has everyone heard the news of Miss Ashford? Or should I say, the new Duchess of Waking?"

Lord Collins stiffened, and Alexa's heart went out to him. "We have heard." Her mother's tone was equally as bland.

"Very good." Lady Chadwick watched Lord Collins like a hawk watches its prey and nodded. "She was a poisonous one." She leaned back in her chair and looked at the sky with a pleasant smile. "It appears the fireworks have started."

Alexa turned to find the most colorful sky she had ever beheld. The lights were deserving of an artist's canvas, but her limited skill with watercolors could not do it justice. She sighed and leaned back.

The slightest scent of mint drifted to her on a breeze, and her eyes met Lord Collins's. He had touched her mere moments before, but his touch could not compare to the effect his words had on her. He had spoken so sincerely, she found it hard to doubt him. But if that was the case, could he actually find her attractive?

Her heart snagged in her chest, pausing its rhythmic movement to slam hard against her rib cage. She loved him. Again. Unbidden tears sprang to her eyes, so she tilted her head and gazed into the night sky. She did not want to love him. Not so she could suffer the delusion that he might like her back.

He wouldn't though. She darted a glance from the

corner of her eye only to find he stared at her. His return gaze was emotionless, and she forced herself to focus once more on the display in the sky. She must have irritated him when she expressed her dislike for him. She should not care if she had irritated him, or if he found her desirable. He would never love her.

How long would it take her this time to discover that?

Another flash flew up, and the small fire exploded into a thousand lights that fell like fairy dust to the ground. That one firework was the closest thing she had ever seen to compare to the way a touch from Lord Collins made her feel. In the future, if she wished to remember him, she would return here. After all, the fireworks disappeared as speedily as any attraction he might hold for her. No one should play with fire, and she ought to remember that.

Chapter 7

"Look at what has arrived in the post."

Alexa turned from her seat by the unlit fireplace and faced her mother. Judging by the irritated expression on her mother's face, Alexa could only guess who sent the missive. Ever since the evening at Vauxhall Gardens, Lady Farris remained adamant about her dislike of Lord Edwin and opposed to the very notion of Alexa seeing him, much less marrying him. Not that Alexa could blame her. His announcement that she must pass inspection by his father *after* he proposed was astounding and potentially ruinous.

She had not spoken to Lord Edwin since that night, despite the glorious bouquet of forget-me-nots he sent the next day. While she knew she sounded petty, part of her wished he had sent dog roses. If only to show he cared about her preferences.

She sighed as she faced her mother. Alexa set her book aside and lightly folded her hands in her lap. "Well? What did he write?"

Lady Farris quietly sat next to Alexa and handed over the letter. Alexa read the contents, ensuring her face remained stoic despite her unruly emotions and set the card aside. "I think Lord Edwin understands how important it is I meet Lord Rudgers. Otherwise, I doubt he would host a house party before the season's end."

Lady Farris inclined her head in agreement, and

Alexa turned to stare straight in front of her. Lord Edwin had invited her to attend a house party at his father's estate in one week, which would determine Alexa's suitability as his bride.

Lady Farris's audible sigh overtook the drawing room. She shifted, and Alexa could feel her mother's gaze bore into her. "I suppose you are still considering his offer?"

Alexa picked up her book, attempting to appear indifferent to her mother's intense gaze. "Of course. In his defense, I am sure he never imagined his father would disapprove of me." At least, that was what the note said which had accompanied her flowers.

"I don't like it. I have half a mind to send for your brother."

Alexa bolted to standing. "Please, don't. Just let me decide for myself. Even if Lord Edwin's father approves of me, I might not marry him. Just let me decide. Please."

"I don't know." Her mother frowned.

"I will know by the end of the house party. I just…" Need more time with Lord Collins.

Lady Farris sighed. "You were allowed too much freedom as a child, and now you are too headstrong. I shan't guarantee we will allow the match, even if you wish it."

"He has been an ideal suitor up till his unfortunate statement at Vauxhall Gardens. Please, give him a chance."

Her mother pursed her lips and considered Alexa. With a shake of her head, she said, "If that is what you desire." Lady Farris stood and moved to the doorway but stopped with her hand on the knob. "A part of me always hoped…"

"Yes?" Alexa prompted as her mother's voice trailed off in a whisper.

Her mother gave the softest laugh and said, "I know it is absurd, but I had hoped you and Lord Collins might…" Shaking her head, she sighed. "Just understand you have other options, Alexa."

The tension seeped from her body as her mother departed. Alexa slumped into the settee cushions with a groan, her hands shaking from the words her mother imparted. Those words had caught Alexa unguarded and almost managed to tear away all semblance of control over her fragile façade.

For truly, her mother's wish was ridiculous. A strange dream that would vanish in the light of day. Of course, a mother would always place more importance on her own child than normal society, so Alexa could excuse her mother's delusions, but realistically, Lord Collins would never find her suitable. Alexa did not possess the beauty a lady must boast to catch Lord Collins's attention.

He required someone willowy with perfectly coiffed hair, and if his too-shallow preferences made him blind to what lay beyond the outer façade, then he did not deserve a truly good lady. He himself could not boast perfection, and she needed to remind herself of that.

She stared at the words on the pages in front of her. Each letter remained a blur, but she did not make any attempt to read. Her thoughts were too far inward for that. Lord Collins was indubitably not meant for her, but Lord Edwin was someone she could marry, if she could only bring herself to say yes. Lord Edwin may be a bit obtuse, but he was an attractive, unattached male in good standing with society, and she would be a fool to pass him up.

She would just have to put Lord Collins from her thoughts, although it was hard to forget him when he said kind or flirtatious things to her. She simply needed to look at his treatment of others to reaffirm her reason to dislike him. It should be easy enough.

****

The rain fell in a dreary tattoo all day. Alexa had to admit she appreciated the coolness that accompanied the dampness. Her hair, however, did not express gratitude, as it seemed to respond to the humidity by rebelling against every tactic her maid used to tame it.

She patted down her boisterous brown curls once more and exited the carriage. Lord Edwin would also attend the Cartworth ball tonight, and he would not approve of the effect the humidity had on her appearance in the slightest. The rain had a mind of its own, though, and she could hardly reprimand it to make it stop.

She scoffed at the absurdity of her thoughts but schooled her features when her mother swung a questioning look at her.

Standing in this rather long receiving line only gave her time to think. She would prefer not to dwell on the notion that Lord Collins might be in attendance. His presence did nothing but provide her with distraction from her main purpose, which was to determine if Lord Edwin was the one for her. And Lord Collins tended to make her doubt that idea.

Maybe Lord Edwin's house party would set him in a favorable light. He swore he preferred the country, and perhaps he would be infinitely more likable there.

It was all so very confusing. Her thoughts continued to shift, and she doubted she could come to a conclusion without further interaction with him.

The receiving line melted behind them, and several gentlemen approached Alexa to request a dance. She floated through the sets and almost managed to ignore Lord Edwin's incessant use of the dreadful word *perfect* and his endless chatter about his father. All in all, her evening had passed almost pleasantly, until she spotted Lord Collins. His eyes bespoke his mood, and she prepared herself for a grumpy encounter with him.

"My lord." She curtsied and smiled at him, attempting to chase away some of his gloom with her cheerful welcome.

His steps stuttered, but he recovered without the smallest of changes to his face. "I thought we might talk."

"Then talk."

"Outside," he said as his eyes flicked over the surrounding lords and ladies.

"You seem to have an affinity for balconies, my lord." She forced the smile to remain on her face despite his obvious impatience and said, "If you desire to speak with me, either sit with me inside or dance with me. I do not wish to go outside." She might not care if Lord Edwin approved of her hair, but she still had her pride. The humidity was not kind and had already made her coiffure frightful enough.

He acquiesced and escorted Alexa to a couple of neglected chairs nestled in an alcove. Several candles rested on a shelf and cast a soft glow in the space, playing off his tawny hair while casting them in shifting shadows. He surveyed the people in front of them and said, "Balconies are the most interesting place at a ball."

Alexa arched her eyebrow at him. "And why is that?"

He brought his gaze to hers and smiled. All movement around her stopped as she once again realized why she could not forget him. Those infernal eyes. "A ball is much too crowded to be interesting."

She gestured around her. "There is almost no one within earshot of us." In fact, it felt as if they were in their own world, right in the middle of a crowded ballroom.

"Yes, we are lucky." He tugged at his collar and gave her a ghost of a smile. "Also, the air outdoors is cooler."

When she remained silent, he inclined his head at her. "Your gown is lovely."

Alexa's heart constricted at the compliment. She had never felt more feminine than when she wore this particular gown. The material was a pale lavender which boasted the most charming ivory lace trim. She hated to admit it, but she had worn it with Lord Collins in mind. "Thank you, my lord."

His gaze went to her hair, and she could not help but reminisce on Vauxhall Gardens. He had expressed interest in her hair on two occasions now. Did he approve of it tonight, despite the moisture in the air? When his gaze lingered, her heart thumped. He just might.

She suddenly felt overheated. She pulled out her fan and gave it a vigorous swish.

He stood and asked, "Would you care for some

champagne?"

She nodded, and he snatched a couple glasses from a footman. He handed her a long-stemmed flute, and she partook of a deep, satisfying drink. The liquid spread its relaxing warmth through her, and she could almost convince herself this was an amicable conversation between friends. "Thank you for that. I needed fortification."

"Against what? Lord Edwin?" His eyes darkened as he resumed his seated position next to her. "I am sure anyone would if they were forced to deal with him as often as you."

She raised an eyebrow and swished her fan. Never mind. This was not a pleasant chat in the least. Based on his compliment of her gown, she had thought he was going to behave nicely, maybe even likably, but they had regressed to this.

"How does a purported stickler for perfection choose to pursue a lady rumored to be a bastard?"

She raised her fan and swished it again. Her cheeks heated, not from embarrassment but from anger. He needed to stop mentioning her supposed illegitimacy. She leaned toward him, beating her fan once more in an attempt to cool her hot temper, and said, "He did not approach me at the beginning of the season. In fact, few did. Not until Miss Ashford, or rather Her Grace, returned to London and helped me."

"She did *what*?" he asked as he straightened in surprise.

She waved her fan again and smirked. "I bumped into her several months ago at a shop. She seemed different, more subdued, and she helped me dispel the rumors about me that she started."

His eyes turned flinty at her words. "Well, she owed you much more than that. The damage she could have caused…"

His voice trailed off, and she grimaced. "She did do more than that. She also helped me choose a better wardrobe." She fingered the lace on her skirt and looked at him. "I cannot say it made me look that much better, but it certainly helped my confidence."

"Why would your confidence need reinforcement?"

Her attention shifted away from him where she caught sight of her mother. "Some people are very thin, and others, such as myself, are not. Her Grace's intervention helped me to accept my curves."

He frowned. "You would not have had to accept your curves if she had not hurt you."

Her eyes flew to his, and she attempted to hide the pain his words caused her. He could at least try to avoid displaying his contempt of her current figure. "She told me gentlemen prefer curves, but I suppose, if you do not, then she said that to comfort me."

His gaze left hers and drifted over her body. She was seated, but she still felt as if he inspected every inch of her. "No, she was correct."

Her heart soared. He could not possibly know the effect those words had on her, but she would cherish them always. "Thank you for confirming that for me, my lord."

He cleared his throat and shifted away from her. "Have you changed your mind about Lord Edwin?"

Her heart plummeted back to reality, and she swished her fan. Lord Edwin never seemed to leave her alone, even when he was not present. "I thought you had decided I should not marry him."

"Yes, and it would behoove you to listen to me, but I know you have not."

"You know me too well."

He nodded in agreement. "I have half a mind to write to your brother, and if he does nothing, remove you from London myself."

"What?" She almost shrieked her response.

"Do be serious. He is not the sort of gentleman you should marry."

"But I love him." She grew better at her lie every time she said it. Although, she didn't know if she should be proud, or chagrined.

"Love." His countenance darkened as he shook his head. "Love does not leave a lady ruined because one's father disapproves."

"He wouldn't have ruined me." She flicked her wrist, sending a cooling gust of wind to her hot skin. "Why do you think he first started courting me? Because everyone approves of me."

"Oh, come now. Edwin's an idiot." She waved her fan, and his eyes narrowed on it. "He doesn't even have the bollocks to stand up to his father, not even for love."

She glared at him and flicked her wrist again. She could hardly argue that logic, so she would remain silent and cool herself. As she continued to use her fan, he eyed it and snatched it away.

"What was that for?" Her hands itched to reacquire her fan, but it was too far away to obtain without making an unladylike spectacle of herself.

"You keep beating away with your fan every time you are irritated with me. It is annoying, so I confiscated it."

"I do no such thing!" She forced a smile as a couple of matrons strolled by and then leaned in to say, "It is terribly unchivalrous of you to allow me to overheat because you are annoyed."

He smirked and opened her fan. Then, he began to wave it in her direction.

If she remained immobile, she could feel the barest of currents on her skin. "Do you think that is useful?"

He must because he beat the fan for several moments longer. His ridiculous method of cooling her did not deserve more mention, so she raised a condescending brow and shook her head.

He snapped the fan shut and placed it in the pocket of his navy-blue evening jacket. His eyes held a twinkle as he said, "There. I tried to be chivalrous, but you just have to be difficult."

Her lips parted in shock. "I can't say your attempt even approached chivalrous."

"It counts." He appeared convinced of his argument. Arguing with him would do nothing. He was too block-headed.

He patted his evening jacket pocket and said, "I heard a rumor of a certain house party you might attend."

The dratted man had just stolen her fan and evidently planned to keep it, but he wished to discuss Lord Edwin's house party? "Lord Edwin has indeed invited me to an intimate party so I may meet his father."

Lord Collins swore under his breath. "Couldn't you just say no before the house party like a good little debutante?"

Alexa gasped. "Like a good little debutante? I shall have you know that this good little debutante has every intention of saying yes."

"Of course you do." He glowered and stood. His size was intimidating as he hovered above her. "When are we to attend this little gathering?"

Alexa lifted an indignant brow. She could never admit she did not wish to marry Lord Edwin, not when Lord Collins continued to insist upon it. "I do not believe it is a 'little' gathering, and when did you receive an invitation?"

"I am going in your brother's stead. Of course I am invited."

She stood as well. "Well, I do not want you there." Except she did. Oh, so badly.

"That hardly signifies."

She had reflected on the outing to Vauxhall Gardens and realized Lord Edwin had behaved extra annoyingly at the dinner table. Lord Collins had asked Lord Edwin questions that seemed to emphasize Lord Edwin's irritating habits, and then she had recalled their walk in the gardens. Miss Cannis and Lord Collins had spoken in secret on the path. Miss Cannis must have told Lord Collins all the things that irked Alexa.

She tried to appear menacing in return, but that only caused a charming grin to grace his lips. "You look adorable when you try to intimidate others."

She growled, and he had the nerve to laugh. Irritation mounted within her that he would not take her seriously. Her fan would have been useful right now, but he had taken that from her too.

Rather than wave her fan, she thrust her hands on her hips. "If you must go, you have to promise to behave."

His grin broadened. "In what way?"

"Every conceivable way."

He *tsk*ed and cocked his head to the side. "Do be realistic. For instance, am I to abstain from all spirits? Or perhaps you insist I retire early each evening."

"Of course not. You must behave yourself in regard to Lord Edwin and me."

"When haven't I?" He pursed his lips, his eyes shining innocently back at her.

"At Vauxhall." His eyes widened in surprise, and she huffed her exasperation. "You know as well as I that you know more than you ought."

He chuckled. "You will have to be more specific."

She ground her teeth. He had a knack for purposely acting obtuse. "You know the things that annoy me about him."

"Who?" He scratched his head, and she grew more annoyed. What was the matter with him tonight? It was almost as if he were…playful. More like his old self even.

"You know perfectly well who I speak of." She sat back down in the uncomfortable, unpadded chair. "Miss Cannis must have informed you what irritates me about Lord Edwin, and if you attend the house party, you will use that against me."

He sat beside her once more and stretched his long legs out before him.

"This is not a game, you know."

He nodded as all the mirth receded from his eyes, replaced instead with somberness. "Yet you did make this into something of a challenge. Do you not recall telling me you would prove me wrong, and then claiming Lord Edwin as your prize? From where I sit, I do believe you will lose this battle."

She scowled. She could recall those words, even if she did not wish to right now. "There are more ways to win this than to convince you."

"Of course there are." He patted her hand, and Alexa felt the condescension in his tone like the prick of a needle. "Your options are limited, my dear. If you cannot gain my approval, then nothing will come of this obnoxious courtship."

Of course there was one recourse she could resort to. But would she want to? She reclined in her chair and crossed her arms firmly in front of her. How was it his words seemed to bring out her defiant nature, every time?

He *tsk*ed, although the gleam of appreciation in his eyes as they dipped down belied his note of disapproval. "Pouting does not improve your demeanor, although it certainly emphasizes your bosom."

She gasped and uncrossed her arms. "How dare you?"

He brought his gaze back to hers and shook his head. "At least that was a better attempt at reprimanding a forward gentleman."

Her eyes grew to slits in her anger. "I have never once failed to take a rude gentleman to task. I'm not sure why you cannot get it through your thick skull that Lord Edwin did not make untoward contact with my person." Because while he had come close, he had not touched her. She inhaled a deep breath and expelled it slowly. She had had enough of him. "And who said I wouldn't reprimand you?" She stood and hissed, "You have no right to note my bosom, and you certainly have no right to instruct me on my reaction to your impudent behavior."

"Oh?" He was also standing, just as manners dictated.

"I may not be able to impart physical damage on your person, but I still have one card I have not played which will put you neatly back in your proper place."

"Which is?" He appeared bored by their conversation and even had the audacity to pull his watch out to check the time. He placed it back in his breast pocket and quirked an eyebrow at her.

Self-preservation told her not to speak, but she could never listen to logic when he behaved in such a vexing manner. "I will run away with Lord Edwin, despite your tricks and orders not to." The words were out. She could not take them back, no matter how much she might regret them later.

Chapter 8

His countenance turned serious and calm, which was not a good combination. "Until he realizes his father does not approve. Then, he will leave you, and you will be ruined."

Her lips parted. There was that.

He laughed softly, although his smile did not reach his eyes. His voice was a silken whisper, sliding over her skin in a dangerous caress as he whispered, "As you can see, you have less power than you think."

Her gaze faltered under his intensity, and she shuddered. "Why? Why do you do this?"

He inhaled a ragged breath. "Because you deserve far better than him. You deserve a man strong enough to realize you are the greatest treasure of them all."

If she was so precious, wouldn't Lord Collins have realized that long ago? Wouldn't he be the one pursuing her instead of Lord Edwin?

Numbness descended on her, chasing away all doubts of Lord Edwin. "Thank you for that, but contrary to your beliefs, Lord Edwin is a fine catch. One my family approves of."

"That may be, but your family will have very little say if I take matters into my own hands."

"And what would that entail?"

His eyes flashed his cold anger. His lips twisted into a smile, and he leaned toward her. "I shall compromise you and wed you myself."

She gasped, her hand reaching up to the base of her throat. She did not want him under those circumstances. Why, her heart would break every time he was forced to exchange pleasantries with her. She would know he did not love her. She would be his obligation.

"I think it best you return me to Mother now."

"Of course." He led her from the alcove as if nothing had transpired between them, not that anything technically had. As usual, her love affair with him was one-sided.

"And return my fan to me."

"When you deserve it." His eyes met hers, and she stopped walking.

He yanked her to him, out of the path of a dancing couple.

She gasped as his arm encircled her waist. She would have been knocked over by the pair if he had not thought to intervene. And that would have been a dreadful scene. She tilted her face up but froze when she saw him. His gaze was locked on her lips, and she parted them. He was so handsome, with such an appealing scent.

Suddenly, he tore himself away and propelled her forward. "Be careful where you stand."

No, she could never resist him if he attempted to compromise her. The briefest of conversations with Lord Collins set her pulse to racing and left her with a tingling sensation throughout her body. Even now, his strong, silent presence did ridiculous things to her insides.

All those feelings were quelled when Alexa spotted Lord Edwin next to her mother. He looked unhappy to see her with Lord Collins, but they were not engaged yet, and Lord Edwin had no say with whom she spent her time. He smiled as she neared, but that smile did not quite reach his eyes. Instead, they appeared cold, like the ground frozen in winter.

"Lord Edwin." Lord Collins smiled cheerily. "I hear you are to host a house party at your father's estate. Was my invitation lost somewhere?"

Lord Edwin raised a disinterested brow at him and said, "It would be impossible to lose an invitation that was never in existence."

Lord Collins scratched his head and asked, "Did you not desire Miss Farris to attend?"

"Of course I do, which is why she received said invitation."

Lord Collins chuckled. "Surely you remember Lord Farris asked me to watch over Miss Farris in his stead. If I do not attend, neither shall she."

Lord Edwin glanced to Lady Farris for confirmation. She smiled and nodded. She obviously enjoyed the altercation, as evidenced by the intent gleam in her eyes.

Lord Edwin's hand went to his pocket and slipped out his silver snuffbox. He took a pinch and then said, "Your presence would ruin the house party. The numbers would be uneven."

"Might I suggest you invite Miss Cannis, then? Your party would greatly benefit from her addition."

Lord Edwin considered Lord Collins's suggestion and nodded. "So be it, but I will not send you an invitation. You can rely on Lady Farris for the pertinent information." At this, he held out his hand in a silent invitation for Alexa to join him.

As Lord Collins released her, his hand caught hers and he bowed deeply. He placed a long, seductive kiss on her palm and smiled up at her. Alexa's cheeks heated as the tingling in her hand ignited once more. She could not imagine what had caused Lord Collins to kiss her hand just then.

She had no idea, until she turned to Lord Edwin and saw the unmistakable glare on his face. Lord Collins already worked quite smoothly to separate the two of them.

"My lady." Lord Edwin offered his arm and smiled down on her. "I believe you granted me this dance."

"Of course, my lord." Alexa moved to join Lord Edwin's side but was dismayed to note Lord Collins had not released her hand. She jerked her gaze up to Lord Collins before returning her gaze to their conjoined hands.

"Your hair," he murmured as he brought his hand up to her proper, confined curls. "I believe this strand was meant to be loose." He removed a tucked away piece from behind her ear and allowed it to float down her neck.

Goosebumps trailed from the spot just above her clavicle where his hand grazed her skin. He held onto her, and her gaze met his in a moment that shut out the world around them. His blue eyes darkened, and he took one solitary step toward her but caught himself and stopped.

"Extraordinary," Lady Farris murmured, which also released Alexa from the spell woven around her.

She turned from Lord Collins and almost tripped over her own feet in her rush to escape. Lord Collins seemed to have lost himself in the moment with her, but how was that possible? He did not want her to marry Lord Edwin, but that did not mean he should behave the jealous lover. Lord only knew what had overcome Lord Collins, but whatever it was, it was not good for her heart. Of that, she was certain.

Alexa drifted away on the arm of Lord Edwin, and Maxon bit back a curse. Something about her compelled Maxon to tease her, to make her feel the same strange, gnawing feeling he experienced every time she was near. He patted his breast pocket, relishing the feel of her fan against him. He should not have stolen the thing, but he congratulated himself nonetheless. Her vexed look at his actions made him smile, for now he knew she felt the same sweeping irritation he felt.

"I do wish you could convince Alexa not to marry him."

He swung around to find Lady Farris standing paces away. She bit her lip as she watched the couple dancing, her eyes filled with worry.

"I will do my best." He slanted a wry grin her way. "Of course, you could tell her no. You hold more sway over her than I."

"I know." She appeared sad, exhaling a heavy sigh. "But I don't know if I can ruin this for her. She seems to like Lord Edwin." She shrugged. "The way I see things, if she still wants to marry him after the house party, then Gavin can intervene."

He nodded. Her plan was sound. Why should Maxon or her mother break Alexa's heart when Gavin could?

"We need to find a gentleman to replace him."

His head jerked in agreement, his gaze never

wavering from Alexa's flowing frame. "She says she prefers blonds."

"Did she now?" Lady Farris laughed. "I should think our search simple enough. Why, Lord Fieldsworth is blond and eligible."

Yes, Lord Fieldsworth did indeed have blond locks. Too bad he had no sense of humor. "No, he will not do."

"What about Lord Parring?"

Alexa switched partners, and he allowed himself to stop monitoring her. He turned to Lady Farris and shook his head. "No."

The light in her eyes struck him as odd. She did not look put out by his negative responses, instead she appeared gleeful. "And why not?"

"Too short."

Her grin widened, but he cut her off before she could speak further. "Enough. I will notify you once I determine a suitable match for her."

"Very well." She still appeared much too pleased about something, and Maxon did not like it. She scanned the crowd and said, "I believe I see Mrs. Cannis. If you will excuse me." She paused, and turned to look at him. "You know, Miss Cannis might benefit from your attentions."

He gave a short bow. "Of course, my lady." He turned to find Alexa back in the arms of Lord Edwin and shook his head. She was a problem. No wonder Gavin had unloaded her at the first opportunity.

Turning on his heel, he went in search of Miss Cannis. Shy wallflowers were not his first choice of partners, but she had a lively mind once she used it, so why not make an exception?

He spotted her along the wall, surrounded by empty chairs. He walked straight up to her and bowed low. "May I have the next dance, my lady?"

She started in surprise and blushed. Whatever she had been thinking about was not in the ballroom. "Of course, my lord."

He led her to the outskirts of the crowd and waited for the current dance to finish. Alexa danced admirably, alternating between partners as if she floated. He couldn't look away, although he should.

Her dancing did not hold him, though. So, what did?

Those lips. That hair. Her figure. He groaned. How had he never noticed her before? Sure, at the start of the season he had enjoyed her company, but he had been too preoccupied to see the lady she had turned into. She could make him chuckle when he should be serious.

Did she make Lord Edwin laugh?

Somehow, he thought not.

"Shall we?"

He almost jumped but managed to remain impassive. He had completely forgotten Miss Cannis at his side.

He led her out onto the dance floor, determined to act as engrossed with Alexa's friend as he could. He would smile and laugh, even if she did not say a word. The orchestra struck up a song, and he led her along the intricate steps.

"What became of this gentleman of yours?" He swore Alexa had mentioned something on the matter the other day.

"I believe he rejoined his ship."

"So I really did muddle matters for you, didn't I?"

She shook her head. "If he had been truly interested, your snub would not have swayed him."

He laughed loudly as if she made a witty rejoinder. She looked at him as if he had lost his mind, and he leaned toward her to whisper, "Paste a smile on your face, whether you are happy or not. I'll be damned if I cause you any more trouble." He darted a glance around, and sure enough, people watched them with avid interest. Lowering his voice, he said in a husky whisper, "I am sorry about your suitor."

She blushed and took a step back, precisely as any young lady should react to an overly attentive gentleman, and he grinned at her. "Well done."

Her lips parted but then twisted up in a small smile. She nodded and said, "Thank you, my lord."

Yes, she was not a lady of limited faculties. He switched partners once more and made sure his eyes lingered on her as she drifted away. If she did not receive positive attention after this, well, he did not know men.

He continued to chat with her, occasionally laughing and allowing his hand to linger on hers for a fraction of a second longer than he ought. And this way, he could keep his mind off Alexa, who danced on the other side of the ballroom. Yes, he welcomed any distraction.

The dance concluded, and he led Miss Cannis back to her seat. As she moved to sit down, she smiled up at him, although something about the glint in her eyes struck him as odd. But then she spoke, and he understood. "We have the same goal, so I believe it would be remiss not to mention he just led Alexa onto the terrace."

His heart rate accelerated. It was bad enough Alexa spent time with Edwin in the ballroom, but she did not need to go anywhere else with him. His hands clenched, and he forced a smile back at Miss Cannis. He would not lose his composure, no matter how desperately he wished to run to Alexa's rescue. Smoothing his features, he bowed over Miss Cannis's hand. "I will come by later for another dance, if you permit it."

"Of course. You know where to find me."

He nodded, turned on his heel and headed straight to the terrace. He did not care that busy, well-lit public areas were deemed safe places for young ladies. In fact, he cared for very little except she now stood there with him.

He entered the cool night air, expecting to see Alexa in any number of compromising situations. Instead, she stood in a corner, alone. He stopped. Had Miss Cannis fibbed?

"Where is he?" he asked, his words clipped. His stomach was doing it again, clenching in an aggravating way at the sight of her.

"Whom do you refer to?" she asked as she turned to face him.

She was so calm. Always so calm. Except for when he irked her. He should irritate her more often. "Lord Edwin, of course."

"I imagine he is in the ballroom, although he could have gone to the cardroom. I am not quite certain."

"Well, why are you out here alone?"

She smiled wickedly, her voice lowering with a seductive quality she should not know to employ. "Would you prefer he be here with me, alone?"

Devilish woman. "Of course not. I would prefer

him gone."

"Excuse me, my lord."

Maxon swung about to find Lord Parring with two glasses of lemonade. Moving aside, he scowled as the blond gentleman joined Alexa. The too-short blond gentleman. Although now that he inspected him further, he was still two inches taller than Alexa.

No, the bloke still would not do.

"Did you need something, my lord?" Alexa asked, lifting the glass to take a dainty sip.

"No." He paused. That response would not suffice. "Err, yes. I thought to tell you all damage to your friend has been rectified."

"Oh." Her lips parted in surprise, and she recovered with a smile. "Thank you."

He gave a short bow and turned away to face the rail. The rain had stopped, but the humid night air still stifled him in an uncomfortable manner.

Perhaps he should blame the weather for his discomfort, rather than Alexa.

But that would not do. In fact, he could not deny his twisted desire to make her as aware of him as he was of her. Yes, she would grow angered by his unnecessary presence out here, but he would relish her response. Because then, he might succeed in driving away her companion, irritating her, and then chasing her anger away with whatever means necessary.

Bollocks, he was pathetic.

He peered over at the couple only to find Alexa acting almost…shy. She was all pretty smiles and demure looks. The poor, wretched man had no idea of her true nature. Her true nature which appealed to Maxon like no other. He welcomed her quick rejoinders. He needed her to take him to task.

She met his eyes, and he tore himself away. He could not stay out there, although something in him told him never to leave. That wicked urge told him to drive away any gentleman who moved too near her, touched her too much. He would go, for his own sanity, before he did something he would regret.

Chapter 9

Days flew by without even a note from Lord Collins. Alexa swore she did not miss him but couldn't avoid searching for the frustrating man at every event she attended. He should never have agreed to watch over her. If he had not returned to London and reentered her life, she could very well have been engaged and happy. Assuming, of course, Lord Edwin's father gave his blessing.

"My lady, are you paying attention?"

Alexa was not the sort to daydream, but she had awoken much too early and could not quite gather her wits about her. She blinked and shook herself. Lord Edwin would not appreciate honesty in this situation, so she kept her response simple and nodded.

He accepted her nod and continued speaking. "The guest list has grown into a perfectly respectable house party, although I would have preferred Lord Collins not require an invitation."

Alexa sighed and picked at her food. "You could have told him no, my lord."

"But at what cost?" He scowled. "If I had not extended an invitation, you would not have been granted permission to attend."

There *was* that. Lord Collins knew how to sway her mother. Although Alexa would likely have convinced her mother to allow them to go without Lord

Collins. But such an excursion seemed rather pointless without him.

Alexa took a final bite of her roasted quail and set her fork to the side. The dining room lacked in ventilation, and the smoke from all the candles burned her eyes. "Perhaps we could take a stroll, my lord?"

He agreed and led her from the dining room, back into the ballroom. Most of the guests still ate, so the ballroom was relatively free from hindrances. He paused by an awning adorned in pure white lilies and took a pinch of snuff. His snuffbox was inlaid with silver and exhibited a Romanesque picture of a beautiful woman with curly hair and classic features. It was remarkable in its design, more remarkable than anything Alexa owned.

She gestured to the box and said, "That is lovely, my lord. Wherever did you acquire it?"

He puffed out his chest and pocketed it. "My father sent for it from Italy. It was a sort of coming-of-age gift."

"He chose well. Is your brother's similar in looks?"

His countenance darkened, and he looked away. "It is best we do not speak of him."

Alexa shifted in the uncomfortable silence. She had heard his brother, Lord Thornwick, was a bit of a wastrel. The mood of the evening had declined, so she lightened her tone and smiled. "I was happy to hear you agreed to invite Miss Cannis."

"It was not like I had much of a choice." He reached back into his pocket and took another pinch of snuff.

"Did you not just take some? Why are you getting more?"

He frowned. "You may nag me when we marry but not before."

Alexa started at his rudeness. She had not intended to nag, only to understand his motivation. It was not as if she had tried snuff before.

He turned to lead her around the ballroom where a growing number of people now circulated. The marble tiles flew beneath her feet, and she counted the cracks in the floor to avoid him. His behavior was touchy tonight, but Alexa was not the sort to walk on eggshells around a gentleman and would not begin now. She squared her shoulders and swiveled her eyes back to his. "My lord," she offered hesitantly, "I know you claimed snuff to be very popular. Is it something ladies partake of?"

"No." His tone brooked no argument. "Snuff is not for women. You must be perfect, so do not ever make such a suggestion again."

Alexa stopped walking. They stood in the far corner of the ballroom which contained the least number of people, although there were enough onlookers to notice an altercation between them. His actions tonight warranted a public scene.

She had tried her best to make polite conversation with him, but he refused to emerge from his black mood. She was thoroughly fed up with him, and she allowed her anger to show on her face. His eyebrow lifted as he turned to face her.

"My lord," she hissed. "I don't know when you decided it was your right to dictate my actions, but I will not stand for it. My behavior is far from unacceptable."

A strange, twisted look entered his eyes as his face

105

hardened into a stone mask. He took a threatening step toward her but stopped. Instead, he leaned in and whispered in her ear a promise that sent a cold shiver down Alexa's spine. "I would advise you to reconsider your words. You will be my property someday. While I generally treat my possessions with respect, I also know how to use a lash to great effect."

His eyes conveyed his sincerity. Alexa hastened away from him. "There will be no marriage between us, my lord."

He sneered down on her. "You will change your mind."

"Oh?" Alexa itched to smack him but controlled herself by gripping her second-favorite fan. Tight. "This is likely the last time I shall speak to you."

"What a shame. I had thought I might invite a certain sailor to my little party. Or would you begrudge Miss Cannis her chance at happiness?"

He had artfully backed her into a corner, and he knew it. The blackguard. "Very well, my lord. I shall attend, but I have made my final decision. We are finished."

He smiled, took her hand in his and placed a gentle kiss there. "A little tiff is only natural, my dear. I am sure I can change your mind."

She shook her head. He ignored her dissent, cradled her hand in his, and placed another kiss on her person, this time on the inside of her wrist. "You needn't worry that I will hold this moment against you. I can be a very forgiving man."

Her lips parted, and she exhaled. "Why me?"

"Because you are as near to perfection as any lady can be, and you will be mine."

Oh, how she truly, inexorably, hated that word.

They resumed walking, but Alexa seemed to tense further the longer he stood beside her. She should turn on her heel and depart his company, but she was too much of a lady. So instead, she decided to vex him in return. "Tell me about your brother."

He didn't even bother to look at her as he said, "I already told you as much as I will about him."

"Do you, or do you not, wish me to marry you? I deserve to know the sort of family I would enter in to."

His eyes smoldered, and he exhaled. "Fine. The last time I saw him, he was in a hellhole in Seven Dials. From what I hear, he drinks himself into a stupor every night. I doubt if he has much longer to live."

No wonder he did not wish to speak of his brother. How tragic. "I am sorry to hear that, my lord."

He shrugged her hand from his arm. "I am used to it. My father is the one that cannot come to terms with it. He will outlive his heir unless my brother stops his drinking."

"So why doesn't he?"

"It is not that simple, my dear. A person like that…well, doesn't care for food or water, only more of his drink."

"Oh." She searched his face. His features were schooled, but a tension to his mouth betrayed him. How must it feel to know your own brother will die and there was nothing to be done?

"That is why I insist on behaving above reproach. My father does not deserve two degenerate sons."

It all made sense, his obsession with the word perfect, his desire to please his father, all of it. Her heart went out to him, but it was too late. He had already ruined his chance with her. "You are a good son, my lord."

He turned her to walk in the direction of her mother, and his lips turned up in a twisted smile. "See, there is one more reason you will wish to marry me. I will be a marquess someday."

"What a macabre thing to say. A title makes no difference to me."

"I know, which is precisely why I need you. You are completely without artifice."

His words caused her to flinch, strangely enough. She did not wish to marry him, but she still felt for him. His story of his brother was tragic, and made her want to offer him solace. After all, she could not deny her nurturing side, which dictated she give him comfort.

The memory of his promise to beat her returned and crept into the small pocket of warmth she held toward him. She must squash his belief they would marry. Immediately. "Thank you," she replied with a twinge of remorse for her blunt answer. "But I can never marry a man who would lay a hand on me."

They approached her mother, and he stopped to whisper in her ear. "I would never. I was caught up in the heat of the moment. You are much too beautiful to damage." Then he led her the rest of the way to her mother, bowed to the ladies, and left.

His words sounded correct, but Alexa did not believe him. The truth had presented itself in the hardening of his eyes when he admitted his willingness to use a lash on her. The man was not trustworthy, and she suddenly felt grateful that Lord Collins would accompany her to Nettleridge.

Chapter 10

The gray sky had hung low and dreary all day, with cooling rain falling on Maxon for the entirety of his ride. He should have ridden in the carriage to this bloody house party, but he needed to finish some business in town and had sent his coach, along with his clothing and valet, earlier. He appreciated a good ride when the weather cooperated. Today was just not one of those days.

The sky began to darken as night approached. He rode up the long drive to Nettleridge, the trees swaying on both sides of him, framing him and granting him no chance at escape. Soaked to the bone and in a foul temper, he still took the opportunity to observe an unhampered view of the estate.

The enormous main house had been constructed at different periods in time. Whoever added the second half of the house had not bothered to combine styles. While one half was gothic in architecture, the other was modern. Even the paint did not match. While part presented as cream, the other displayed a wretched muddy brown. All else appeared in good upkeep, and quite pleasant to behold with many mature trees surrounding it, and green lawns stretching out before it.

As he continued his ride to the estate, he cursed under his breath. He should not have come. He should have convinced Alexa to spurn Lord Edwin's advances, but he had failed. He couldn't even blame Alexa for her unfortunate choice. Love made one blind to all manner of failings.

While he would not allow the match, he also could not break them apart. Something deep within him forbade breaking her heart, even if her heart did not break for him. His stomach tensed at the thought, but he brushed his reaction aside. Some ridiculous part of him wanted her to like him, maybe even love him. Instead, she disliked him, and it hurt.

He entered the stables and chased away his irrational, self-centered thinking. The stables welcomed him with their cleanliness and eager grooms. One groom took Tyr, while another prepared some oats and water. Once Maxon verified Tyr's well-being, he hurried to the house. A wizened butler led him to his room where his valet, Chaney, awaited him.

"It is about time you arrived, my lord," Chaney greeted as he helped Maxon from the wet overcoat.

"It is good to see you, too," Maxon said with a smile. In his opinion, the upper-level servants could get away with a bit more familiarity, especially his unparalleled valet.

"It started raining about an hour into our trip. When it did not let up, I feared you would have to stay at an inn tonight."

"It was not so bad," Maxon said as he undid the buttons on his sodden navy waistcoat.

"Your attire suggests otherwise, my lord." Chaney turned to the armoire and pulled out a change of garments. Maxon could only grin in response. He was soaked through and ought to bathe but could not seem to bring himself to do anything other than change and search out a nip of scotch.

Shrugging from the waistcoat, Maxon turned to the bed where his clothes now awaited him in a neat pile. "Sometimes, I think you deserve a raise." The clothes looked so dry and welcoming.

"You won't hear any arguments from me, my lord."

Maxon chuckled and continued to peel away the wet garments from his chilled skin. The warmth from the fire dried him as Chaney helped him into his change of clothes. He would have to bathe in the morning before he saw *her*. Granted, he might behave better if he did not smell like his normal pleasant self.

Because, truly, he needed to mind his manners. By whatever means necessary.

His responses to her had veered too close to flirtatious while in London, which was precisely why he had avoided her for a full week. Until now. Now, he would have to monitor her and protect her from Lord Edwin.

Damn these house parties.

The last time he had been at one, he had commenced courting Miss Eleanor Ashford, now Her Grace, the Duchess of Waking. His interlude with Miss Ashford had seemed idyllic, but the more he thought about the past, the more he suspected the lady had executed an expertly planned illusion. Not that she somehow forced him to experience nonexistent feelings for her, of course. Rather, the lady's true personality did not match her façade.

And now, Alexa swore the duchess had changed, but how could he accept that? People, especially women, did not change.

Except for Alexa. She had changed into a bit of a shrewish creature. He supposed he deserved some hostility but not outright dislike. Her dislike stung enough that he could not clear it from his mind. He wanted her approval—no, he needed her approval.

He turned to the dresser where her fan rested. His valet had considered it most unusual he insisted the fan accompany them, but he thought it best to return it to her, in person. Where he could tease her.

Chaney began to arrange a cravat at Maxon's neck, but Maxon ended that bit of nonsense. "That will not be necessary. No one is awake, and if they are, they cannot expect my cravat to be in place."

Chaney shook his head and stepped away. "Very well, my lord. Is there anything else you require of me?"

"No. Thank you."

Chaney left without making a sound, and Maxon turned to the dresser. He never went anywhere without his watch fob. After all, it was his most tangible memory of his father. And why should he part with something that belonged to the man so unfairly ripped from his life?

He slipped it into his pocket and sighed. While tired, he also thirsted, but he would have to depart his room to find the smoother scotch. The best scenario he could hope for entailed sneaking into the library, having a drink alone, and returning. Unobserved. His hope was unlikely, but he could still dream.

A few wall sconces remained lit, even though the majority of guests were in bed by now. He rounded a corner and stopped at the dark doorway to the library. He had enquired as to its location on his way to his chambers. Based on the butler's directions, this must be it. The closed door would not budge when he jiggled the handle, but his attempt prompted a loud thump coupled with a muffled curse to emit from within.

After a few moments, the door swung open, and a pretty blond maid exited. Her hair fell sideways in a state of obvious disarray, and she jerked her bodice up as she stopped in front of Maxon. She managed to give him an inviting smile as she curtsied and then continued on her way.

"Oh. It's you," Lord Edwin said with a frown.

"Did I interrupt something?"

"No. At least, nothing you should concern yourself with," Lord Edwin said, leaning back further in his armchair.

Maxon scowled and went to the decanter filled with scotch. The room suddenly seemed unwelcoming, despite its cheery yellow walls and multitudes of books. "You dally with servants?" He tried to appear unconcerned as he filled a glass, but inwardly, his blood boiled.

Lord Edwin chuckled. "She is more of a mistress than a servant."

And yet Lord Edwin acted as though his response epitomized normalcy. "Does she reside here, or at your estate?"

"At my estate, of course."

Of course? Keeping a mistress at one's abode defied convention and cast Lord Edwin in a rather lackluster light. "And when you marry? What will she do then?"

Lord Edwin tensed, and he gave Maxon a wary look. "Why should I answer to you?"

Maxon quirked an eyebrow and sipped his scotch. No true gentleman preyed on the servant class, and no gentleman would keep his lover under the same roof as his wife. Alexa would never marry this man if he had any say in the matter.

"You should answer to me because you need my permission to wed Miss Farris." He downed his drink and helped himself to some more. How Alexa dealt with this man sober floored him. "I doubt Miss Farris would approve of your dalliance, either."

Lord Edwin waved his hand. "Women are much too delicate to understand such matters. I would be doing her a favor by keeping Henrietta in my household. There are certain things a gentleman does not do to a lady, although I could be wrong about Miss Farris. Just the other day she suggested she try snuff. Naturally, I silenced that upstart notion."

Lord Edwin held standards much too strict for Miss Farris, and the idea that he should keep a servant around to sate him was ludicrous. "I do not think you understand, Lord Edwin. Neither I, nor Lord Farris, will countenance the idea of you marrying Miss Farris, under any circumstances."

Lord Edwin's gaze met Lord Collins's and held for several seconds. He leaned forward, and a gleam entered his eyes. "Why don't you admit you want her for yourself? I can't say that I blame you. With that bosom and—"

Maxon stepped toward him, hoping the bloke would understand the very real threat Maxon presented. "I suggest you stop. I should hate to have to hit you the first night of this gathering."

Lord Edwin held up a hand. "We speak as friends

here, my lord. If you had wanted her so badly, you should have claimed her."

Maxon turned away and placed his empty glass on a side table. "The truth is, I do not want her, but we both know she is too good for you." His thumb twitched, which was ridiculous, because the tightening in his chest should have been betrayal enough.

"There are many who would disagree."

"Fortunately, their opinions do not matter." Maxon left the library. His mood had turned black, but he had nowhere to go but his room. He should have never come down for a drink, although he had learned some pertinent information.

Tomorrow, he would send Chaney to procure a bottle of scotch so he would not have to enter the library again. A drink in his room would do just as well.

He turned as he exited the library and almost tripped over a dark figure crouched on the floor. "Hellfire and damnation," he muttered as he caught himself against the wall in an effort to avoid tumbling over.

The figure straightened, and he cursed again. Of course, Alexa stood before him. He caught her elbow and pulled her against him as his anger welled up within. Without thinking of the repercussions, he growled at her, "Lead the way to your room. Now."

She opened her mouth to speak but he stopped her by saying, "No buts. Just go."

She turned away with a mulish set to her lips and led him down the hall. He couldn't help but notice she stood at a perfect height for him, and she smelled once more of roses. Her pace was remarkably fast for such a graceful walk, and his eyes refused to budge from her hips as they swayed. Despite her voluminous robe, he could see the definite curve of her figure. Lord Edwin had been correct when he complimented her bust, but it did not compare to her hips. They were just so round and lush. He stopped his wayward thoughts. It did not matter how enticing her figure was. This was Alexa.

She turned toward him at her doorway and once again opened her mouth to speak. Maxon had no desire to be seen with her, so he simply opened the door and pushed her in. She almost fell, but he caught her and closed the door behind him. No sound emerged, except for the scrape of the door as it clicked shut in place, and then, the darkness swallowed them.

Alexa gained her bearings in the dim interior of her room before bringing herself to face Lord Collins. She had snuffed out her candles, thinking she would sleep, but when sleep refused to take its hold, had wandered down to the library for a book. The fire still smoldered in the grate, but its light was meager, at best. She could make out the outline of his face, but the firelight distorted his features, turning an already angry expression into a frightening one.

"Why are we in my room?" Her heart skipped a beat. No man had ever been in her room, and the feeling was completely foreign, albeit exhilarating.

He ran a hand through his unkempt hair and sat down on her bed. The mattress groaned as his weight settled. He should not sit there, but he should not do many of the things he did tonight.

"Remove yourself from my bed."

"I will not. I have been riding all day, and I wish to rest."

She scowled at him, knowing full well her back

faced the fire and her features might not be visible to him. "And I would like you out of my chambers, so go."

"Or what?" He tilted his head and smiled, the glow of the fire adding a deviltry to his smirk. "Will you scream? Or perhaps carry me away?"

His callous disregard for her wants was nothing new. How could she expect anything different when he constantly frowned upon Lord Edwin's suit? Her hands itched to push him from her bed, just to expel her own frustration, but she stopped when logic arose. His argument held merit, no matter how callous his actions. She could not scream, unless she desired to face ruination, and his frame suggested he would not budge.

The force of her anger dissipated, and she suddenly felt weary. She had only wished to venture downstairs to find a book but instead overheard more than she ever wished to, or expected. Her emotions still reeled from the blow of both Lord Edwin's complete disregard for her feelings, and Lord Collin's repudiation of her, and now she was forced to suffer Lord Collins's presence in her room. It was all so terribly unfair.

There were no chairs, so Alexa went to the nearest wall and slid down into an ungraceful heap. The wall cooled her heated frame, and she leaned her head against the hard surface, closing her eyes to blissful darkness.

"You will not sit on the floor."

"What other option do I have?" She shook her head and continued to regard her inner eyelids. It was dark, and if she focused all her effort, she could almost forget Lord Collins seated on her bed. His words, however, posed a more difficult obstacle. She could not forget that he did not want her.

"Of course you have a choice. As a gentleman, I cannot allow you to remain there." A soft thumping sound reached her which she could only assume was him, patting the bed. "Come. Sit."

"You cannot force me to sit with you. It is entirely too improper."

His tone suggested his annoyance with her. "What would you consider my presence in your room then?"

Alexa opened her eyes and gave him her most frigid stare. "A mistake." She almost smiled at her own ability to sound unaffected, but managed to stop herself. "A mistake that is entirely unwanted."

The air stilled around them as his gaze sharpened. As much as she would like to return to her inner solitude, she could not close her eyes, not now.

His eyes failed to betray any of his emotions. He was always so bloody unreadable. "Well," he finally asked, "what were you doing on the floor?"

"I was eavesdropping." Her voice was barely a whisper, but to her, they were the loudest words she had uttered in some time. Those words rang through the room, bringing back all the emotions she felt outside of the library when she heard Lord Collins state he did not want her. She could never forget that statement. She had been correct to think Lord Collins would not find her desirable, and now his affirmation would forever remain etched in her mind.

"What was that?"

She exhaled a pent-up breath and spoke louder. "I was eavesdropping."

"Precisely as I suspected. How much did you hear?"

"Enough." At least enough to know he did not want her. She closed her eyes again and embraced the darkness. His words should not hurt her so. She already knew he would never choose her, but still, the thought of his disinterest cut her.

The room remained silent for some time, and then Lord Collins cleared his throat. "I am sorry, but maybe it is best you know the truth about Lord Edwin. He is insufferable."

Alexa laughed at the irony of the situation. He thought Lord Edwin caused her distress. She had determined all on her own that Lord Edwin was an oaf, although his dalliance with a servant had caught her off guard. "Thank you for illuminating that for me, my lord."

"You have yourself to thank for that. You should not have behaved so foolishly."

As if it were her fault the gentlemen acted in such a boorish manner. "I shall remember that the next time I require a book and happen upon two men speaking about me. Loudly, I might add."

He cringed. "My apologies, but it is for the best. Now, we can depart from this cursed event and get on with our lives."

Alexa smiled and shook her head. "Oh, we shall not leave yet." A wicked thrill ran up her spine as her defiant nature took hold of her. "You may deem Lord Edwin unsuitable, but I do not."

"What do you mean?"

She would never marry Lord Edwin, but she wouldn't leave now. It wasn't as if her decision harmed Lord Collins, aside from forcing him to spend a few extra days at a house party. With her. Really, it would be foolish *not* to stay.

"I know how marriages work in the *ton*, my lord. If he was not tupping a servant, he would find someone else to tup." She only knew one word to describe the act married people engaged in, although its meaning eluded her.

"Oh?" he asked, his voice an angry growl. "Who told you these things?"

"Does it matter?"

"Yes, it matters." He ran a hand through his hair and sent her a menacing glare.

She could feel the fury in his voice and grinned. It was delightful to have the upper hand for once. "You and Gavin were loud about your activities when we were younger, my lord." She had overheard more than she ever should have.

He shook his head and scoffed. "You cannot be serious. I would never speak that way in front of a lady."

"But you would in front of your friend's little sister." He shifted and cleared his throat as she sighed. "Oh, it wasn't as if you knew I listened. I just happened to overhear."

"Oh. So you know what tupping entails, then?"

Her cheeks heated, and she looked away. "Of course, I am not a simpleton, although I wonder why males are all so keen on engaging in the act. From what I have seen, it appears a male and female bump against each other for a brief period, and then it ends."

"From what you have seen?"

His voice was elevated, and Alexa rushed on as she averted her eyes from his face. "You know, it is hard not to see the animals tup from time to time."

Suddenly, he grinned. "Do you know another word for the act? Or is *tup* it?"

Her face heated to an overly warm temperature. Luckily, the soft glow in the room was not bright enough to illuminate the extent of her deep crimson blush. "That is none of your concern." Her fatigue made her long for his departure, so she went to stand before him in hopes he might go. Sooner.

His words sounded much calmer as he leaned back and said, "I see. So you know much less than you think you know."

"I know enough, my lord. Now, kindly depart so I may sleep."

He ignored her suggestion and sat there staring at her, his eyes pinned to her hair. "I think you know enough to get yourself in trouble." He exhaled and muttered, "Thank the heavens for chaperones."

She scowled at him. "Yes, because a chaperone managed to dissuade you from entering my room."

"I am not the one you need protection from."

"Aren't you?" She raised her brow in question, but the truth hit her as the words left her mouth. Of course not. Any other lady in the kingdom would need a chaperone around him, but oh no, not her.

"No." His eyes gleamed as he continued to stare at her hair.

He had not moved from his seat. He clearly had not understood her the first time. "If you will excuse me, I must rest."

He did not budge. He offered her the briefest of nods and said, "Of course, I will depart immediately."

Alexa waited, but he just sat there. She raised her brow and crossed her arms over her chest. She itched to tap her foot but held her open display of irritation at bay. "My lord, you must vacate my room."

He rose to standing, and Alexa tensed to find him so near her. He towered over her, and she craned her neck to look up at him. His hand reached out to the side of her head and stroked a tendril. "It is so soft," he said, his words as faint as the whisper on a breeze.

Her stomach performed an erratic somersault, and her mouth went dry. "Thank you."

"You really do need a chaperone around you at all times, you know."

She nodded. She felt alarmingly exposed and vulnerable, even though her nightgown and robe covered her. If only he stood a step further from her, maybe then she could breathe.

His free hand circled to the small of her back, and he drew her to him. He pulled her close until their figures met and a swirl of tension surrounded them. His other hand lingered in her hair and he whispered, "I just don't think you understand. Men are not to be trusted."

She forced a nervous laugh. "Of course I under—"

His mouth descended upon hers and cut off her words. His velvety soft lips explored hers until she parted her own. The invasion of his tongue shocked her, but she welcomed it as tingles raced up her spine. Never had she dared believe a kiss might transpire between herself and Lord Collins, yet here she was, in his arms. His lips were so gentle, and he tasted pleasantly like the scotch he had drunk that night. His smell was a bit different, more earthen, as if he had just come in from the outdoors, but she quite liked it. Her arms came up to the back of his head, and she pulled him closer to her.

His hand entwined in her hair, and she pressed herself against him, hoping with all her might that this moment would never end. His lips burned everywhere they touched, and all she could do was pray she would not get too scorched. Each touch melted her, as if he had practiced such ministrations before.

A tiny corner of her heart shattered. Of course he had practiced this many times. He had a sordid reputation for his way with the ladies, and besides, hadn't he admitted just minutes prior that he did not want her? She shuddered. She meant nothing to him. Nothing.

Alexa turned her head away and fought back the tears that threatened. How could such a moment inflict so much pain? He kissed her jawline, and she said, "You must leave. Now."

His mouth went to her neck, and he nibbled at her collarbone. "Are you certain?"

She squeezed her eyes shut and fought off the sensations he unlocked within her. "Yes." She spoke louder and looked upward in an attempt to control herself. The moisture in her eyes bordered on the precipice of overflowing. "Get out."

He stilled and disengaged himself from her. His clouded eyes cleared as sudden realization dawned. Immediately, he stepped back as if he had indeed been burned. "It's your damned hair. You should hide it away."

Again, pain stabbed her. Was there no end to his cruelty tonight? She turned from him and smoothed her robe in an attempt to regain composure. When her eyes dried, she turned back to him, trying, but failing, to hide the bitterness from her voice. "I am sure my hair forced you to kiss me."

"There is no other logical explanation," he agreed without an ounce of levity.

Alexa inhaled, pressing her hands to her diaphragm to steady herself. "Please, my lord, leave. Just go."

He shrugged, as if their embrace was something he experienced often. "Of course." Striding to the door, he placed his hand on the knob but stopped before he opened the door. "And you. Stay in your room at night. It is unsafe in the dark, all alone."

He opened the door, and she whispered, "And, evidently, it is unsafe with you." Silence greeted her statement as he closed the door, leaving her to speculate if he heard her or not. She sighed and sat on her bed. She supposed she would never know the answer.

Chapter 11

"Uggh," Alexa moaned as she rolled over. The sunlight streamed through her bedroom window in an unrelenting manner that made her quite cross. She considered throwing her pillow at the beam of light but instead buried her head in it instead. Throwing pillows did not satisfy her as much as one might think.

Her bedroom faced the east, so why had her maid not drawn the shades? No one could sleep through this amount of light, not even her. She could get up and pull the shades herself, but it was too late. She was awake.

Several minutes passed with her face shielded from the light, until she flopped over. She gazed at the window and noticed for the first time the dark green color of her walls. No wonder her room seemed so much darker at night. Of course, she had barely registered the darkness, not with Lord Collins in her room.

She shut her eyes and lay there, adjusting to being awake. Normally, she would fall back asleep, but today her thoughts were in a whirl.

He had kissed her last night.

The moment seemed glorious until she recalled his rude words. Then, every semblance of sweetness which accompanied the kiss vanished, replaced with shards of grating glass against her heart.

One's first kiss was not supposed to be like that. It

was supposed to be the equivalent of a dream, the sort that left one longing for more, rather than something best forgotten. Her heart felt heavy, and the worst part was, he could never know just how much he hurt her. She would bottle up her sorrow and stow it away to deal with alone.

She shook her head and went to the vanity. Her lids weighed heavily from lack of sleep, courtesy of Lord Collins, and her hair trailed down her back in a snarled, ashy brown mess. Tea would help her immeasurably. At the very least, it might give her cheeks some much-needed color.

She grasped the bell pull and tugged. One of the maids would arrive soon. She sat on her bed and waited, and then waited some more. When no one answered her summons, she gave up. The household must be overset with demands, so she would have to secure her tea all on her own.

Her own maid would not think to check on her at such an unusual hour, so Alexa attempted to calm her boisterous hair, and then put on one of the only dresses she could pull on without aid. It was a pastel yellow color, and she hated it. The color seemed much too similar to the infuriating sunshine.

She arrived downstairs to find breakfast laid out for the houseguests. She inhaled the welcoming scent of freshly baked bread and smiled. A dainty teacup beckoned to her, and she rushed to fill it with tea before taking a seat in one of the many chairs situated around the massive table. She would break her fast alone in the large room, which suited her just fine. After all, she could not deal with people. Not in her current condition. She lifted her cup, took a long sip, and closed her eyes.

"Surely you do not plan to ignore me."

Alexa's eyes flew open at the deep, rumbling source of her interruption. Before her stood Lord Collins with an impish grin on his face. He looked well rested, and she scowled. Their kiss must not have affected him the way it had her.

She could surmise from his attire that he had either just finished his ride or would embark on one soon. His stiff cravat suggested he had not engaged in physical exertion, but knowing Lord Collins, he would look perfectly pieced together after a brawl with a wild boar.

Her cheeks grew uncomfortably warm as she sat under his scrutiny, so she tamped down her emotions. If he could remain unfazed by their interaction, then she could at least act as if she were immune as well. "Of course not. Why would I ignore you?" she asked, setting her teacup down with a smile.

He raised his eyebrow and ran a hand through his hair. He shifted, and she almost laughed out loud in disbelief. Maybe he was affected, but it was out of shame, not desire for her. He cleared his throat and said, "My lady, would you care to stroll with me?"

"No."

"All right." He inhaled and tried again. "Let me put this plainly. You will stroll with me."

"No, I will not." Nothing good could come from a stroll with him, and it was best he realize it.

"Fine, but we must talk, and I would prefer to speak in private about our kiss. If you wish, we will speak on the matter here, where anyone might stumble upon us."

She almost agreed out of sheer stubborn defiance,

until his words permeated her tired mind. Speaking of such private matters in the dining room would not do at all. "Very well." She glared and muttered, "After my tea."

He agreed, and she continued to glare as she took another sip. Her eyes drifted away from him, and she took in the décor of the room. The giant aged table bore all manner of marks on the surface. Newer furnishings usually boasted much more elaborate lines and finishes than this large, plain table. She looked past him and eyed the tapestry displayed on the wall. There was a scene of a noble lady and her lord surrounded by horses on a lush hilltop. Each wall held similar tapestries, and she smiled at its quaintness.

She looked at Lord Collins once more, and her smile disappeared. He had much to answer for, so why did he appear so content? All he did was lean against the door frame and grin at her. He should have to suffer a little, so she helped herself to another cup and proceeded to take the daintiest sips in all her life. Several minutes passed before she returned her gaze to him. He still grinned in amusement as if he enjoyed standing there, watching her take her tea.

She drained the remaining dregs and stood. She could continue to draw this moment out, but he had accepted her very obvious attempt to annoy him with impressive patience, and she could not fit any more tea into her belly.

"Shall we?"

She said nothing and allowed him to lead her into the foyer. A harried-looking servant rushed by, and Lord Collins stopped him and instructed he follow. Then, he turned back to Alexa and led her outdoors.

The day still shone sunnily. She would have to ensure her maid drew the shades henceforth.

"That was not very nice of you, stealing that footman from his duties. The servants must be in a tizzy with all the visitors arriving today."

"Would you prefer to go out unchaperoned with me?"

"Of course not. So long as the footman does not get into trouble."

"I will ensure he does not."

Silence ensued, and Alexa stared at the ground as it stretched out before her. She ought to have thanked him for engaging a chaperone, but he truly did bring out the worst in her.

"I was impressed to see you up so early, Miss Farris. I have always admired the early riser." Maybe this was why he brought out the worst in her. He said things which contradicted her nature.

Their feet crunched on the gravel path which seemed to continue for a good distance. Large poplars shaded the path which also shielded the sun. Hopefully, Lord Edwin would not see her without her hat outdoors. She did not need him to offer more of his horrid skin cream.

She looked up at Lord Collins to see if he jested about her being an early riser. He did not. "I do not rise until right before noon, my lord. I am not a morning person."

He pulled out his silver watch fob, consulted it, and said, "It is nine o'clock. Why are you awake, then?"

"My room faces east, and the sun would not cease shining." His lips pulled into a tense line. He did not seem to approve of her late mornings, and she bit back a smile. "I do enjoy my rest, although most ladies sleep much later than I."

"Oh?" His voice held disbelief.

"Of course." How did he not realize that most ladies of the *ton* slept well past noon? "In fact, I dare you to name any lady who awakens in the morning hours, on purpose."

They rounded a corner of the house and discovered a pond nestled amongst several trees a short stroll away. She liked ponds, even if this one was a vivid brown hue. He seemed to be leading her unerringly toward it.

"I can name two." He held up two long, elegant fingers and ticked off first his index and then middle finger as he spoke. "First, the newly minted Lady Farris, and second, her cousin."

Alexa scoffed. "You actually believe that about Her Grace? She likely told you that to make you like her."

His eyes shuttered as he stilled. "I think you may be right, but Lady Farris, without any doubt, rises early."

She could concede that, but her new sister-in-law was an aberration. "No one is without their flaws, my lord."

"It is hardly a flaw to rise before noon."

"Why? Because you deem it so? Forgive me for holding a different opinion than you." Oh, he vexed her so. Why should it matter what time she awoke? If she ever had an appointment, she would arrive on time, and then take a nap later.

His eyes remained planted on her until she motioned for them to continue. They started, and the footman resumed walking at his respectable distance, as well. The lawn surrounded them in a stunning shade of green, and she shuddered to note not a garden in sight.

They neared the pond, and a frog leapt from the bank into the water which sent ripples over the otherwise smooth surface. Along the bank, various wildflowers bloomed, so Alexa stooped down and picked one. Several small, deep blue buds rested in her palm, and she inhaled the subtle scent.

When she turned back to Lord Collins, she caught him staring at her with an unreadable expression. She dropped her gaze and continued to meander by the shoreline.

She spoke over her shoulder to him. "Truly, the hours I keep are quite early by *ton* standards."

"But by country standards, they are not."

She arched her brow. "Indeed, but I live in town."

He chuckled. She had not meant to amuse him, but somehow, she had done just that. She continued to walk until he reached out and caught her hand in his. She turned to find him gazing down on her, his eyes holding a grave look that caused her to shudder.

"My lady."

"Yes?" she asked, trying ever so hard to fight off the sparks his touch elicited.

"I wish to apologize for last night. I never should have taken such liberties with your person. I overindulged in scotch, in too short a period, and my judgement was impaired."

Alexa's hand tightened in anger and disappointment, and she tried to draw away from him. She could handle an apology, but couldn't he at least say he desired her? Blaming alcohol was just insulting.

She glanced to her flowers and frowned. The

darling little buds lay crushed and wilted in her hand. They deserved better treatment than that.

For a moment, she could not draw breath, but then she looked in his irresistible blue eyes. She would not accept an apology like the one he had just offered.

"No, my lord." Her voice emerged just short of a whisper.

"I beg your pardon?"

"You cannot blame scotch for your actions. You knew exactly what you did."

She waited with bated breath for his response. His hand went to his watch fob, and he scrutinized it with a blank expression on his face. She coughed, and he nodded, returning his hand to his side and allowing the fob to dangle in place. "You are correct."

"Then why did you kiss me?" She looked away from him in an attempt to hide her emotions. No matter his answer, she doubted her wounds would disappear. Not after he had admitted he did not want her. And why should he? It wasn't as if Alexa could ever compare to *her*.

He scowled and turned his attention to the pond. "Your hair seemed to come alive in the firelight, and I could not help but touch it."

She waited for him to continue, but when he did not, she bristled. "First, you blame spirits, and then, you blame my hair. Why do you not take accountability for your actions?" The sun's rays beat down without mercy. She shivered, despite the warmth of the day.

At her words, his gaze went to hers. He eyed her and took a predatory step toward her. She sensed she had pushed him too far as his voice dropped to a deep, scratchy whisper. "You wish to know why I kissed you? How about because I wanted to?"

Everything fell away, lost to the brute force of his energy. This response was most unexpected.

"There is no other reason than my desire for you." His eyes clouded, and she shivered again. He turned his head from her and said, "I am supposed to be the consummate gentleman, yet I could not resist the one I swore to watch over and protect."

She parted her lips, and his eyes went to them. His normally light-hearted mien held a harsh note, a devilishly uncaring one that made Alexa shudder in anticipation. "I have a great many duties, you know. You are not the only person to rely on me, yet you are the only one I failed." He cursed and took one more step to her, coming nearly toe to toe with her. "It is shameful, but dammit, I want to do it again."

Somehow, he had lost himself to their surroundings. Either that, or he purposefully wished to bring down ruination on her. Because, right now, she knew he would kiss her again.

His lips lowered, and immediate, logic-defying panic overtook her. She might accept his reason for kissing her—after all, it was the answer she had dreamt of hearing—but another kiss was extremely ill-advised. Especially one with a footman present to witness. She took a hasty step back to remove herself from his grasp. He called out to her, but it was too late. Her foot slid on a patch of mud, and she fell back, her arms flailing to catch anything, but of course, nothing availed itself to her.

Her landing was not too hard, seeing as she fell along the bank, and a good portion of her fall was on a mixture of grass and mud. Dangerously near the water.

In fact, one more inch would have ended in a splash rather than a thud.

The cloudless blue sky stared down at her, and she blinked. She should be grateful for her graceless fall. Her body had acted of its own accord, stepping back like that, but now she rather regretted the missed opportunity to kiss him. Reputation be damned.

"Alexa, are you unharmed?" Lord Collins rushed to her side, just as the footman who had hovered a respectable distance behind also joined them.

"I believe so." She accepted the footman's outstretched hand, ignoring Lord Collins's as a small act of rebellion.

She straightened her askew skirts and groaned. Dark brown mud mixed with splotches of green marred her yellow skirts. Even her hands were caked in mud, so she sent an apologetic smile at the footman, whose hand was also now soiled.

"Are you certain? You look a trifle peaked."

She turned toward Lord Collins, who, in his defense, actually appeared concerned. "I shall be fine, once I return to the manor."

"Shall we, then?" Lord Collins bowed, and then offered her his arm as if they attended one of the finest balls in London, rather than standing on the bank of a pond with her so disastrously clad. And her hair. She could feel the weight of it settled on one side, rather than centered on the back of her head as it ought to be. She could not help it, though. Not unless she first unbound it and then attempted to pin it back in place. With dirty hands, no less.

So ignoring her hair, she accepted Lord Collins's proffered arm, and bit back a smile as some of her mud transferred to his jacket sleeve. "I fear I am in need of a bath."

His nose crinkled, and he nodded. "You do have a bit of an odor."

Her lips itched to smile, but she nodded instead. He led her on the most direct path back to the manor which went past the stables, and to an area of the manor hopefully less frequented by guests. The footman resumed trailing after them, and as they reached the stable yard, Lord Collins chuckled.

"You know, I can't say a lady has ever fallen before to avoid my embrace."

"Speaking of which, whatever were you thinking? If I hadn't avoided you by whatever means necessary, your presumptuous actions would have *ruined* me."

He shrugged. "I believe it's fair to say I was not thinking."

"So, what? You were overcome by emotion and couldn't stop yourself?"

"Something like that."

Goose pimples splattered across her arms, preceded by a shiver of excitement. "If you are so easily swayed, I cannot help but wonder how you are not yet wed."

"I assure you I am not typically swayed."

What did that even mean? The implications of his words seemed impenetrably difficult to decipher. Why, that would suggest she had affected him enough he would forget his surroundings in its entirety.

"Just see that you resist insensible impulses in the future."

He nodded. His face remained serene, but she could have sworn his forearm tensed.

How curious. This morning could have turned out

drastically different, and the one to stop a union was her. The person with actual feelings involved.

"If it helps, I was not fond of your dress."

She remembered herself with a start, and found him smiling down on her.

"If anything, I would say the grime has helped its appearance."

Her attire was comical, at best, and something within her broke. Instead of the righteous anger he deserved, she laughed. Out loud, and freely. "You know, I quite agree with you. Your sleeve, also, has improved drastically."

He chuckled back at her, and the most unusual thing happened. The air shifted around them, and she swore she was fifteen again, escorted by the most debonair gentleman she knew. But unlike in her tender younger years, she knew what lay ahead. Heartbreak.

Their steps slowed as they reached the back entry, and Lord Collins disengaged to swing the door open. Surprisingly enough, Lord Edwin and an older version of himself stood there, on their way out. She inhaled and ducked behind Lord Collins in hopes that Lord Edwin would fail to see her.

"Ah, Lord Collins. Out for some air, I see."

Lord Collins moved to the side and, judging by the speed with which he moved, had not even considered shielding her from Lord Edwin. "Yes. As is Miss Farris."

Alexa pursed her lips in exasperation. Of course Lord Collins would not behave the gentleman. Why would he when he benefitted from Lord Rudgers's disapproval?

Lord Edwin surveyed her with a scowl. "Whatever

befell you?" He turned to his father and tensed his lips to an apologetic smile. "Miss Farris does not normally look so frightful. As I told you before, she is typically perfection itself."

He swung his gaze back to Alexa and frowned. Alexa released her skirts and smoothed back her hair, shocked by the severe disapproval in his eyes. He had never looked at her in such a way before.

"Miss Farris!" Lord Edwin said, his disapproval turning to panic. "You just smeared mud through your hair. Are you trying to make matters worse?"

"Of course not, my lord." She bristled. "I did not choose to fall, nor did I choose to be muddied in the process." She turned from him before he could respond, and dipped a curtsy to Lord Rudgers. "Now, if you will excuse me, I should like to change." She then picked up her skirts, smiled to Lord Rudgers, and stormed into the house. Her soiled gown brushed Lord Edwin's leg, and she sent a prayer skyward in hope that some mud had rubbed off.

Alexa scurried away and left Maxon to deal with Lord Rudgers and Lord Edwin. A voice called out from behind him, and he turned to find the footman hovering at his elbow, looking uncertain. He had forgotten all about the chaperone. So he thanked the man and sent him on his way. He turned back to find Lord Edwin regarding him in a speculative manner, so Maxon rewarded him with an upraised brow.

The silence stretched on, until Lord Rudgers coughed. "Well, she certainly could use the ministrations of her maid."

Maxon looked sharply at the older gentleman.

Lord Edwin reddened and hurried to say, "Miss

137

Farris is the very definition of a lady. Please, do not judge her on that one meeting." He turned to Maxon, stuck out an accusing index finger and said, "I do not understand how she fell."

His responding answer was as dry as he could make it. "Well, you see, there was a spot of mud, which she happened to step on. She lost traction and flailed backward into the area by the banks of the pond."

"What sort of gentleman allows a lady to slip?"

Maxon smiled, when really, he wanted to throttle the man. No one questioned his honor. "Obviously a very chivalrous one."

Lord Edwin turned even redder. "You should have never allowed her to fall."

"How would you suggest I go about that?"

"Don't escort her outside in the first place."

Egad, but this was a tiresome conversation. "And deny her access to taking the air? How absurd."

Lord Rudgers said in a bored tone, "You two can stay and sort things out, but I have a ride to go on."

"I will accompany you, Father." Lord Edwin hurried behind on his father's heels, which left Maxon alone.

He smiled as he walked through the halls. Alexa must be furious after Lord Edwin saw her in such a state of dishabille. He could not have planned things better if he tried. After all, if Lord Rudgers disapproved of Alexa, her relationship with Lord Edwin would never come to fruition.

But how could anyone disapprove of Alexa?

She exuded all things sunshine and light, until she became incensed, and then she turned into a summer storm with all its glorious thunder. Her personality had always veered to a more fiery nature, but he knew badgering her would ease her from distemper the fastest. Granted, sometimes that method resulted in the opposite reaction he sought.

And now, he likely owed her another apology.

What had he been thinking? He knew a chaperone stood mere feet away, yet he had thrown all reason to the wind and tried to kiss her. Again. His impulse had seemed too strong to resist, and he should thank the heavens she had taken a tumble rather than marry him.

He entered his room and rang for a servant. He would eat lunch alone and maybe read a book. His chair beckoned to him, so he sat and contemplated the cold coals in the fireplace.

Alexa had every right to call him out. Her glorious, glowing hair might have sparked the inferno of his attraction the previous night, but he had acted on his desires. Her lips had compelled him with their lush and inviting fullness, and even now, he would gladly partake of them again.

He needed to stop his lust, though. It went beyond unacceptable to kiss her, not when he was supposed to protect her. There was just something so tempting about her, although her dislike disconcerted him, and she had fully displayed that dislike that very morning when she prolonged her tea just to frustrate him. That, or she enjoyed toying with him as much as he did with her.

Realistically, she engaged in the former. And what should he expect? She had told him she did not like him, and then he kissed her. Because how else should he respond? He sighed, placing a hand to his weary brow. He needed to keep Alexa from Lord Edwin, and if kissing her accomplished that, he would just have to make the sacrifice.

The sound of howling wind caught his attention, and he glanced at the window. His room faced the gardens, which, ironically, were to the west. He, the early riser, received a room without morning sunshine while Alexa battled the sunshine as she slept in.

Large, gray clouds rolled in, and it looked like it might rain. Maybe Alexa would be able to get a nap without interference from the sun. As a gentleman, he should offer to trade rooms with her. His eyes drifted closed, and he shook his head. She would have to simply remember to draw the curtains at night.

****

Alexa's blood felt near to boiling as she reached her room. How dare Lord Edwin treat her in such an ill-mannered way? Lord Edwin had sent her a reproving glare that set her on edge, but it was the words he said that drove her to outright fury. He had actually said she looked frightful.

She fumed, and with good reason, so she redirected her anger to pacing the length of her room, back and forth. She had already realized Lord Edwin and she did not suit, but she did not know if she could stomach his presence for a full week.

She stilled as she turned around. The sky had darkened to a surly gray hue, and a breeze brought in the cleansing scent of rain. The pond she almost fell into lay outside of her window. It appeared smaller from her elevated position but just as inviting. Tomorrow morning, assuming the rain let up, she would have to take a book out there to do a bit of reading.

That plan only worked if she could take her mind

off Lord Collins though. With his handsome face and smooth tongue, he grew increasingly difficult to ignore. If only her heart would stop beating its loud cadence whenever she thought of him or bumped into him. Her little infatuation with him grew more and more pathetic. He never once said he cared for her in *that* way or thought she looked pretty. No, he used none of the fancy words on her that he must employ on other ladies.

She observed the rain as it dripped from the roof. How strange that she should identify the one droplet amongst the multitude of other raindrops. That one raindrop was so similar, yet so different from the others. Just as Lord Collins was similar to other gentlemen, yet still managed to make her breath catch when she neared him.

She shut her eyes against her sigh. Her growing obsession with Lord Collins was problematic, and she dearly wished she could rid herself of it.

The picturesque view of the pond held her until the servants finished drawing her bath. She smelled of potent pond scum. She would likely fall ill from excessive bathing, but she could not go down for supper in her current state. Essence of rose infused the bathwater, and it smelled delightful. She submerged herself in its warmth and began the process of washing her hair. Now, she would smell like roses, and if Lord Collins continued his odd obsession with her hair, he might catch the barest of whiffs.

Alexa was no martyr, but she had to stay at this house party for Miss Cannis's sake, and maybe, just maybe, she could receive another entirely too welcome kiss from Lord Collins.

Chapter 12

Lord Edwin greeted her upon her descent for dinner. Her maid had styled Alexa's hair in a beautiful, rambunctious coiffure that benefited from wayward strands, and even he would have a hard time criticizing it. That, and her maid had used a staggering number of pins tonight, so hopefully nothing would riot out of its position unless intended to do so.

"You look ravishing tonight, my lady." Lord Edwin bowed low over her hand and beamed at her. Her cheeks heated, and she avoided eye contact by continuing to walk to the dining room. He followed and extended his arm to her. "I cannot help but appreciate your gown. What color would you consider it?"

She glanced down at her pristine white gown. "White, my lord." It was a plain enough, and the color nothing special. She continued to walk, but this time allowed him to escort her.

He looked disconcerted at her brusque tone, but he recovered and said, "I am happy to see you rallied from this morning's unfortunate events."

"As am I, my lord. I do detest appearing frightful."

He stopped their stroll and turned her to him. "Is that why you are upset? Because I said you looked frightful?"

She raised her eyebrow, allowing her tone to sound frosty. "Is there some other reason I should be aware of?"

"Of course not." He patted her arm and smiled at her. "I did you a favor, so there is no reason for you to act cross. If I had not interjected, Father might not give you a second chance to make a good impression."

"I already told you we will not wed." How obtuse was Lord Edwin that he could still believe he had a chance?

"I know." He tucked her arm in his own and began to walk again. "We will, though."

Her free hand clenched into a tight ball. Apparently, he was dense to the point of block-headedness. "What must I do to convince you otherwise?"

One of the other house guests hailed Lord Edwin before he could respond, and she endured a tedious, polite exchange before they finished their short walk to the dining room. "Ah, there he is," Lord Edwin said as he brought Alexa across the room to where his father stood.

They approached Lord Rudgers, who appeared engrossed in conversation with another gentleman. Lord Edwin and Alexa stood in polite silence until Lord Rudgers turned to them and acknowledged their presence. "Father." Lord Edwin smiled. "May I present you to Miss Farris? You may notice she is a bit more presentable than when last you saw her."

Lord Rudgers raised a quizzing glass and inspected Alexa at length. She fought back the desire to squirm as she waited for him to finish his intense perusal of her person. "Yes, she does look better."

She froze. What an asinine thing for the marquess to say to her. Should she smile, or perhaps say thank you? No. She refused to do anything more than nod.

Lord Edwin apparently knew what to do, because he laughed and said, "She most certainly does. One might even say she looks perfect."

"I don't know if I would say that. She is beautiful, but perfection is difficult to achieve."

Lord Edwin nodded and appeared to ponder his father's statement while Alexa tried her best to avoid displaying any emotion. What an ass. The old adage must be true: like father, like son. Another guest caught Lord Rudgers's attention, and Lord Edwin led her to the table.

Lord Edwin chose a spot near the head of the table and helped Alexa into her seat. She slid into her chair and smiled at the other guests present. Some still mingled, but most already sat around the behemoth of a table. She did not recognize many of the others in attendance, except for Miss Somers. She would have to write to Laura and apprise her of Miss Somers's whereabouts.

Lord Edwin patted her arm and began to converse with someone next to him, while Alexa prepared the letter in her mind that she would write later.

The remaining guests sat, and the servants brought out the first course. Alexa tasted the dish, a green asparagus soup. It tasted utterly delectable, so she ate a fair amount.

She had eaten it much faster than a lady ought, so she smiled politely and set her spoon to the side in hope no one would notice. No one paid her the least bit of attention, and she relaxed.

Her hands rested on her lap as she searched for the one gentleman she most wished to see. Suddenly, her stomach lurched as her gaze landed on him. He sat next to Miss Cannis and looked devilishly handsome in his stiff evening wear. His light hair, while tousled, did not appear messy. Overall, he looked exactly right.

He picked up his water goblet and looked her way. He winked at her, and then returned his attention to Miss Cannis. That wink did not mean anything to him, but it certainly had the power to make her mouth go dry. She picked up her own goblet and sipped some water. She had forgotten herself. While she did not wish to marry Lord Edwin, she still had to convince Lord Collins she did.

A light garden salad arrived next, so she took a bite and turned to Lord Edwin with a smile. "Nettleridge is lovely."

He set his fork to the side and nodded. Still chewing, he said, "It is, isn't it? I obviously prefer my estate, but you must wait to see it on a later date."

"When shall we tour your estate?"

He paused to think before saying, "We must wait on the weather. It is raining tonight, so I do not think tomorrow advisable, but perhaps the following day?"

She started to agree but stopped when Lord Rudgers stood and commanded the attention of the crowd. "Ladies and gentlemen, thank you all for joining me at Nettleridge. I think you are all aware of my love for music, so I am demanding a concert after dinner each night. Aside from those events, well, you can figure that out for yourselves. Nettleridge will not disappoint so long as you give her a chance." He then sat, and the room erupted in a smattering of applause.

Once the din died down, she took another bite of her salad. Lord Rudgers turned to her and asked, "Do you play the pianoforte, Miss Farris?"

She swallowed and inclined her head. "I do, my lord, but only tolerably."

"How disappointing," Lord Rudgers said as he sipped his wine. "Will you play tonight?"

"I will, if you desire it." His attention started to turn elsewhere, but that would not do for her plans at all. She needed to convince Lord Collins she had charmed Lord Rudgers so she said, "Lord Rudgers, if music is your passion, I would suggest you hear Miss Cannis play."

He swiveled to her and leaned forward. "Oh?"

Alexa sipped some more water. "If she were a man, she would have been a concert pianist, my lord."

He exhaled. "Which one is she?"

Alexa motioned toward Miss Cannis and caught Lord Collins's steady gaze on her. Her plan had worked. He appeared unhappy with her as he sat there, watching her with hawk-like scrutiny. "She is the lady in the pastel purple gown, my lord. Her strongest passion in life is the pianoforte."

Lord Rudgers smiled and turned to Lord Edwin. "I do not recognize her, so she must be your guest. You have done well, son."

Lord Edwin beamed at him, and Alexa ate the rest of her salad. Even if she did not win over Lord Rudgers tonight, she had still made Lord Collins believe she had. She turned to look at him and grinned. His blond brow arched, and he looked away in an obvious snub. She frowned and took a final bite of her salad. He should have responded with interest, not anger.

The servants brought out the next course, and Alexa's stomach lurched. She hated prawns with a

146

passion. Delicacy or not, they turned her stomach.

"Are the prawns not divine, Miss Farris?"

Of all the times to single her out, it had to happen now. She smiled and began to prepare the morsel. Several people, including Lord Rudgers, watched as she pulled the head off and removed the outer shell. She bit into the soft flesh and nearly gagged. After choking the offensive thing down, she looked up and despaired at the sour look on Lord Rudgers's face.

"These prawns are by far the best I have ever eaten. No wonder you love them so, Father," Lord Edwin said.

Everyone diverted their attention from Alexa, and dinner resumed as usual. Lord Edwin leaned over and whispered in her ear. "Prawns are his favorite food. You could have at least *acted* like you enjoy them."

"I tried." She frowned and focused on her plate. The damn prawn's head faced toward her, and she swore it looked at her with sympathy. Water would not cut it tonight. She beckoned over a footman, and he poured her a glass of wine. The auburn liquid numbed her tongue, and she closed her eyes, savoring the bliss it brought.

Another course appeared, and she almost expired with relief when presented with roasted quail. She ate at a ladylike pace, and did not quite finish before the next course arrived. The footman whisked her plate away and replaced it with a lemon custard. Each bite tasted like heaven must, but when the servant brought out a chocolate mousse, she almost groaned. Her already sated appetite demanded she cease eating, but who could resist chocolate? She ate a spoonful and almost moaned out loud.

She looked around to make sure she had not made

a sound, only to find Lord Collins looking her way. He watched her with an amused grin on his face. He pointed at his chin and she raised an eyebrow. He then smirked and pointed at her. Her hand went to her chin, where, much to her dismay, a spot of chocolate rested. Her napkin cleaned the rest of the mousse off, and she mouthed a silent thank-you to Lord Collins. He inclined his head and returned to his own dessert.

Lord Edwin leaned toward her and said, "There is still one more dessert. If you continue to eat your mousse, you will look piggish."

Alexa's cheeks heated, and she set aside her spoon. Lord Edwin was a blockhead. Who served three desserts and expected the guests to only eat a little of each? She glanced back to Lord Collins and caught his expression before he masked it. He pitied her, as if he understood she had just been chastised. Her appetite fled from her, so she waited through the remaining dessert, sipping on her wine and planting a demure smile on her lips. Then, when the other ladies rose, she accompanied them to the drawing room to select music for the concert.

Her heart felt heavy and did not allow her to enjoy the musical portion of the evening, although she usually appreciated all forms of entertainment. Several people performed, and then it was her turn. She sat on the bench in front of the pianoforte and began to play. Her fingers flew across the ivory keys in a perfectly respectable rendition of her favorite composer, Haydn, and when she finished, she rose and curtsied. Everyone applauded, and she sat down.

Miss Cannis played next and silenced the crowd with her skill. She threw herself into her performance, and Alexa could almost feel the passion in the notes. The music was sublime, and at its end, everyone rose to award her a standing ovation.

"I think it best we end the evening on that note," Lord Rudgers said as he took the stage. He held his hand out for Miss Cannis. She accepted as he offered an ingratiating smile to her before he addressed the crowd once more. "I do not believe anyone can outshine Miss Cannis, so it is best we adjourn. Until tomorrow, everyone." He then turned to Miss Cannis and began to speak in earnest to her.

Alexa rose and headed for the door. Lord Edwin snared her arm on the way out, and he pulled her into a darkened, empty corner of the room. His eyes hardened on her as he towered over her. "You were correct, my lady. You do play tolerably."

Her shoulders sagged, and her lips parted. She was no musician, but surely her abilities did not deserve such censure. She stopped her negative thoughts and smiled at him. "No one can fault me for my skill."

His grip on her arm tightened, and he whispered, "Maybe, but you will have to do better than that if you are to impress Father."

She quirked an eyebrow. "And yet I still have no reason to impress him."

He turned his back on her and disappeared into the crowd. Tonight's events had dealt more than enough of a blow to her spirit, and she longed for bed. She left the drawing room and returned to her own room, feeling very much alone.

Chapter 13

Alexa crossed the damp green lawn, raising her skirts in an absurd effort to avoid any lingering moisture from yesterday's rain. She held her book, a thrilling guide to gardening, in her other hand. The overcast sky should safeguard her complexion, but she wore a large-brimmed hat just in case the sun peeped out.

With the help of her maid, she laid a blanket on a slightly drier patch of grass under the shade of an oak tree and sat down. Her maid had experienced these outings many times, and knew to lay another blanket down nearby for her own enjoyment.

The water lapped at the banks of the pond, and she tried to clear her mind by reading her gardening book. She loved roses, and one day, she planned to plant an enormous garden full of them. She continued to read in tranquil silence, until a flash of color forced her attention away from the book.

Miss Cannis walked toward her with a contented smile on her face. When she drew near, Alexa patted the blanket and smiled.

Miss Cannis sat and said, "I saw you from the window and thought you might enjoy some company."

"You were correct." Alexa marked her spot in her book and set it to the side. "Have you seen your captain yet?"

"Was I supposed to?" Miss Cannis's brow furrowed in confusion. "I believe his ship has been called away, so he could not possibly attend."

Alexa gasped. "You cannot be serious. The only reason I am here is because Lord Edwin promised to invite him."

Miss Cannis arched an eyebrow. "I am sure Lord Edwin did invite the captain, but I would wager he never expected the captain to accept."

If Alexa had not already determined to deny Lord Edwin, this would have been the final strike against him. How conniving, and utterly deplorable.

The wind rustled the tree above her, and Alexa nodded in rueful acknowledgement. "You must be right." She growled and straightened. "He is so very frustrating. I cannot stand him, but at least he kept his promise by inviting you."

"It is a very nice party so far." Miss Cannis's eyes narrowed and she asked, "But what is this about you not being able to stand him? Does that mean you are finished with Lord Edwin?"

"Yes, but please do not tell Lord Collins. I am keeping it secret." Miss Cannis nodded, and Alexa added, "Lord Edwin is convinced he shall change my mind about marrying him."

"Of course he is."

They both laughed. When the laughter died down, Miss Cannis sighed, her eyes clouding over as if her thoughts ran wild miles away. "And what of Lord Collins? You haven't fallen for him again, have you?"

"No." Her response issued forth a little too quickly. She longed to confide in her friend but expressing her emotions out loud would feel too forlorn, too melancholic. "He acts in my brother's stead. Otherwise, he would not even be here."

"Oh." Miss Cannis sounded disappointed, which meant her friend believed her lie. Her acting passed muster, after all.

"I do have an interesting story for you, though."

"Ooh, do tell." Miss Cannis leaned forward as Alexa proceeded to divulge the previous morning's fall. Naturally, she left out the part about Lord Collins's kiss from the night before, and his desire to kiss her again.

Miss Cannis wiped a tear from her eye as Alexa finished her story and laughed. "You fell in the mud. I love it. And I fear I support Lord Collins's decision not to shield you when you met Lord Rudgers. I would have done the same thing, not to embarrass you, but to try and end this absurd relationship between you and Lord Edwin."

Alexa shrugged. "As I said, I don't wish to wed Lord Edwin, so I am not overly upset. Granted, I would prefer to earn Lord Rudgers's disapproval by my typical behavior, not from having muddied skirts."

"Yes, but I cannot imagine you would warrant such a negative reaction unless something drastic occurred. Face it, you are eminently likable."

"Yes? Explain that to Lord Collins. I daresay he would disagree."

"I don't know about that. He speaks highly of you."

This certainly came as a surprise.

The day had warmed, and the clouds dissipated. Miss Cannis stood, smoothed her skirts, and smiled down at Alexa. "I am afraid I must return indoors. Lord Rudgers implored me to perform something of a solo concert tonight. His piano is quite impressive." She exhaled and her eyes grew unfocused. "I have never played on so fine an instrument. Each key was perfectly tuned, and I cannot wait to play on it again."

Alexa grinned as Miss Cannis waxed on. She tended to get sidetracked when she spoke of music. "It is about time someone recognized your skill. I am so proud of you."

"Thank you." Miss Cannis blushed and waved before turning toward the manor. Another breeze rustled the trees, and Alexa picked up her book to read about her roses once more.

****

The previous night had almost driven him crazy. Every time Alexa leaned toward Lord Edwin, Maxon had wanted to tear her away from him. Then, when Lord Edwin had so obviously reprimanded her, Maxon had been forced to hold himself back from sauntering over and punching the bastard in the face. But what had Alexa done? Nothing but sit there with an imbecilic smile on her face and accept Lord Edwin's criticisms.

His morning ride had not sufficed to erase her from his mind, so now he walked. Of course, his feet took him to the one location where he could think of nothing but her. He rounded a corner of the manor and took in the view of the pond. The glassy water sparkled in the morning light. Nary a cloud marred the sky, and now the sun beat down, having erased the dew from the grass long ago.

As he neared the pond, his eyes narrowed on a colorful lump underneath a tree, with a second lump to the side. He would prefer not to deal with people and had almost turned around when he identified one of the lumps as Alexa, who slept soundly and appeared very much like a sweet, docile young miss. Quite the opposite of her true nature.

He tore his attention to the other lump, or more precisely, Alexa's maid, who also slept. A competent chaperone would not fall asleep, but then he would not have the opportunity to approach Alexa as he did now. He grinned and crept toward Alexa, doing his best to avoid disturbing the prone figures in his approach.

Ever since his return to London, she had acted grumpy, but her icy façade had melted. He wanted things to return to normal, just as they were in their younger years. Relaxed and easy. Simple, and uncomplicated by this infernal longing to draw her to him.

And now, her undeniable magnetism seemed amplified as Maxon gazed down on her. A wayward curl, which moved with every breath she took, lay planted on her full lower lip. Her soft exhales were audible from where he stood, which implied she nestled in a dream state.

The incessant, ever-present desire to kiss her flashed across his mind, but he shoved that notion aside. Why, he considered her a little sister. Under his protection. And in broad daylight with a sleeping chaperone nearby.

Yes, he ought not to kiss her.

So instead, he knelt beside her and plucked a green blade of grass from the lawn. He could not resist such enticing lips, so he started there. He ran the blade of grass lightly across her lips, and then once more, until she uttered a soft moan and swept at her mouth.

He chuckled and waited for her to settle before he

leaned eagerly toward her. This time, he tickled her nose, which resulted in a cute little snort and another swipe of her hand. Her hand fell back, and he leaned forward with alacrity but suddenly stopped himself. What was he doing out here? He would never, under any circumstances, act in such a juvenile manner toward another lady.

Alexa was different. Yes, he found her attractive, but mere outer appearances did not set her apart. Simply put, he actually *liked* her. He enjoyed her company and her looks, and now he feared she had managed to snag his heart. No wonder her desire to wed Lord Edwin bothered him so. He would never wish Lord Edwin on any lady, much less one he liked.

A frog croaked near the pond, and he started. He could not condone his budding feelings for the lady. No matter what, Gavin would disapprove, assuming matters progressed as far as matrimony. Women did not deserve his trust, not even Alexa. No. He would not countenance anything with Alexa, no matter how tempting.

He sat back on his heels and considered returning to the house. He had to behave as he normally would, so he gave in to his desires and leaned over her once more. This time when he brought his little blade of grass to her delicate nose, her eyes flew open and she gasped. "My lord, what are you doing?"

Her allure pulled him to her, but her eyes held him with an inescapable draw. Sleep clouded them, and even more striking was how sweet and vulnerable she appeared. Very gently, he pulled the dark hair from her lip and smoothed it to the side.

She blinked, and her eyes gained focus. "Is this a

dream?"

"Would you like this to be a dream?" His words sounded husky to his own ears. She appeared exactly how she might look waking up beside him in bed.

She said nothing and continued to stare up at him. Long thick lashes framed her eyes and enhanced their blue color. They contrasted beautifully with her porcelain skin.

At least, her skin *had* been porcelain.

"How long have you been out here?" he asked as his heart began to thump in his chest. He should have returned indoors, not stayed out here, tempted by this vixen.

She blinked. "Not long. Why?"

He sat up and immediately regretted his hasty action. He had been more than content to remain planted above her. He inclined his head toward her. "You have turned a light shade of pink."

She gasped as she sat up and straightened her askew hat. "Please, tell me you jest."

He shook his head. "I am afraid not."

She pointed at the tree above her and frowned. "What happened to my shade?"

"The sun tends to move, my lady." She must have slept for a long time, because the shade seemed quite far removed from her current position.

Her dour look transferred to him, and he chuckled. "It is not so bad. You are only a trifle pink."

His words must not have reassured her, because she stood and turned to the manor. "I believe I should return. I would hate to darken further." She shuddered at the notion, and he scrambled to stand.

"It is a beautiful day. Why not stay out here with

me?" He regretted the words the moment he said them. He needed to stop giving into his foolish impulses. It would be best for all involved if she left.

She tilted her head to assess him. The sound of a nearby lark filled the silence, jerking her to face the source of the sound. The lyrical music died away, and she turned once more to face him. "Fine, but we must move to the shade. And what happened to my maid?"

He jerked his head toward the servant, who had managed to nap in the shade, and said, "She appears to have succumbed to the same impulse as you."

"Oh, right. I can't say this is the first time we have slept outdoors."

He hid a grin at her response and picked up the blanket, moving to spread it over a patch of grass under the same shade the maid used. Alexa sat, and he occupied the space beside her. "How does one manage to nap as often as you?"

She grinned, and his heart stuttered. Her pert nose crinkled in an adorable fashion he had never appreciated until now. They were seated side by side on the small blanket with luscious green grass surrounding them, and both were careful not to touch.

"I think I could sleep anywhere. A good nap is not something one should take for granted."

"Of course," he agreed in mock seriousness.

She peered up at him from beneath her thick lashes. "Don't tell me you are the sort to never nod off."

"I am afraid I am guilty as charged." Although he had napped the previous day. That was out of character for him, though.

"Of course you are." She shifted, and he could not

help but appreciate her delicious curves displayed next to him. "You must slide between silk sheets on a pillowy mattress during the day. Then, you will be forced to appreciate naps as much as I do."

He blinked. Did she attempt to flirt with him, or did she truly feel so strongly about slumber? As Gavin's little sister, she must mean the latter, but who could pass up such a delightful opportunity? "If they were your sheets I was sliding between, then I am sure I would agree. Granted, I don't think I would be able to nap."

She arched her brow in question. "What else would you do? Read a book?"

He stilled. He should never have said those words to her, but at her suggestion, he found it difficult not to envision himself in her bed. With her. "Yes," he said, holding his breath to observe every detail of her expression, "I would read." She accepted his statement without even a twitch. Disappointment filled him. She had not attempted to flirt with him, after all. "What are you reading?"

She lifted the heavy tome from her lap and handed it to him. He flipped through the pages as curiosity filled him. "I had no idea you enjoyed gardening."

"You know very little about me, I think."

He stilled. How strange to think he had spent many holidays with her, but he did not know the most basic information about her. "Do you garden often, then?"

Her grim look transformed to a smile. "Oh, yes, as much as possible."

"How do you manage in town?"

She made a sour face and said, "It's much more difficult. Mother allows me the back garden so long as we are not entertaining. She claims I become too dirty to receive anyone, and thinks it best I should hide myself if need be."

That was understandable. No one received calls with dirt under one's nails. "How sizeable is your garden at home?"

She bit her finger and looked around. "I would say it is at least double the area of the pond. Maybe even a little larger."

He tried to imagine her garden and nodded as the picture formed. That would be a sizeable garden indeed. "How do you manage such a large endeavor?"

"I do all the work, but sometimes I enlist the aid of a footman. Mother grows quite incensed when she sees me all covered in dirt, but it is worth it."

Her face lit up with excitement, and he handed her book back to her. The image of her in a soiled gown amongst a burgeoning garden came to mind and he grinned. "I can only imagine how fulfilling that must be."

"The feeling is parallel to none, my lord. To see one's hard work come to fruition." A hint of color from her excitement stained her cheeks, and her eyes expressed her joy. "Imagine planting a seed and watching that seed turn into a plant that eventually flowers. It is remarkable, to say the least."

Her excitement lightened his own mood, and he laughed in a light, carefree manner. "It sounds exhilarating and messy. Just your sort of thing."

The light in her eyes dimmed, and he regretted his words. Her eyes went to her hand as she fidgeted with the gauze on her skirt. "I try so hard to behave the perfect lady all the time. Lord Edwin expects it, but look at me. I end up sunburnt, and my favorite hobby involves dirt."

No one should make her feel this way. Once more, Maxon felt the urge to punch Lord Edwin well up within him. He scowled and looked at her. "Perfection is overrated and boring."

She scoffed in disbelief. "Tell that to Lord Edwin. He values nothing but perfection."

"And that is why he is an idiot." He frowned. "You cannot possibly believe you would be more interesting if you were perfect all the time, can you?"

"I don't know."

Maxon placed his hand over hers. A spark of anger had lit within him. How could she not know her own worth? "Well, you would not be more interesting if you were perfect. In fact, I doubt I would like you very much."

She scoffed. "I remember Miss Ashford. She was perfect, or at least, she acted like she was, and you fell for her."

She spoke the truth. He had loved the very perfect-seeming duchess. How then, did Alexa's imperfections appeal to him so? In fact, he appreciated them most about her. The truth of the matter hit him, and he said, "You are correct. I did fall for her, or at least, I thought I had fallen for her." A small, white butterfly floated by only to disappear into the leaves of the tree overhead. "I don't think I knew her. She hid herself from me and presented me with a false image. I loved the idea of her, not the lady herself."

"Oh." Her words lacked conviction, and when he looked at her, he could tell she did not fully believe him.

"Think back to the night in your room when I kissed you." She blushed, and he said, "I kissed you because I found you attractive, irresistible even. Your hair framed you, set alight by the embers of your fire, and you were adorned in a worn dressing gown. You were the loveliest in that moment."

The color drained from her face. Her stormy eyes looked enormous as she asked, "What is your point?"

His eyes held hers, and he leaned into her until they were mere inches apart. "My point is I kissed you. I never kissed the duchess."

Her lips parted, and her eyes dilated. The way her face tilted up to him offered an unmistakable invitation, but the sheer desire in her eyes truly pulled him to her. Ever so slowly, his lips lowered to hers, and the most glorious feeling of rightness overtook him. He did not care how they knew one another; he only knew she held the power to erase his troubles and pain.

The lilting song of the lark returned, and he pulled away as realization hit him. She could inspire great joy for him, but she also held the ability to hurt him, and hadn't she stated she disliked him? Could he allow such heartache to transpire?

She removed his hand from her shoulder and stood. She said nothing, only smoothed her skirts and moved to her sleeping maid's side. With a gentle shake, the maid awoke, and the two strolled back to the house. He scowled as she receded from view. He found her nearly irresistible. How had that happened, and why did he not seem to mind?

Chapter 14

Alexa and her mother descended the grand staircase for dinner. She had chosen a demure cream gown for the evening, which revealed neither too much nor too little. Her curly brown hair rested atop her head, secured by midnight blue ribbons which matched the ribbons tied beneath her bosom and the slippers on her feet. Tonight, she dressed for her own happiness, and no one else's.

"Oh! There is Mrs. Cannis. Will you be terribly upset with me if I leave you here?"

Alexa inclined her head and waved her mother on. "I will be fine. Don't worry about me."

Lady Farris left Alexa to attend to her friend, and Alexa strode to the sideboard. Sherry before dinner would be just the thing, especially after last night. She doubted she could face another dinner without suitable fortification.

"Are you certain sherry is a good idea?"

Alexa jumped from the surprise of Lord Edwin's voice behind her. The liquid in her glass sloshed, and a trickle made its way over the edge. She turned to face him, and his gaze drifted to the honey-colored spot on her otherwise pristine glove.

His dour expression appeared overly harsh, but he did not reprimand her. He surveyed her, and she squirmed when his eyes landed on her sunburnt skin.

Her eyebrow lifted, and she brought her glass of sherry to her lips where she proceeded to take a defiant sip.

"I thought we might chat."

"Of course."

He steered her to a quiet corner just outside of the dining room and asked, "Wherever did you get such a horrid burn?"

She sighed. Her fair skin had changed to a light shade of pink, but she looked positively dark compared to the other fair-skinned ladies. "I fell asleep outside."

He shook his head. "You must behave above reproach henceforth, my lady, but with that burn, you might be too late. Father has begun to form a poor opinion of you."

She brought her index finger and thumb to the bridge of her nose and shut her eyes. While she ought to commend him for not using the word perfect, he still failed to comprehend she would never marry him.

"Are you well, my lady?" he asked with a touch of concern.

She inhaled and looked him in the eye. "Yes, my lord, although I would feel better if you stopped thinking I wish to impress your father."

His eyes hardened. "You keep saying you do not wish to marry me, but I will change your mind, and when I do, it is best Father approves of you."

"I assure you, there is no changing my mind."

He ignored her, fishing in his pocket for his snuffbox and then inhaling a small amount. "I think it best you do not sit near Father tonight. He serves prawns at every meal when he entertains, and I cannot bear to see that face he made again." He eyed her again and said, "Also, if you sit further from him, he might not notice your complexion."

"Fair enough." She did not truly wish to sit near Lord Rudgers or Lord Edwin.

Suddenly, a searing pain scorched her right shoulder, and she gasped. She looked down to find candle wax on her skin. She stepped away from the wall to avoid future drips from the open wall sconce, and Lord Edwin followed. The wax had cooled almost immediately when it hit her skin, but it left behind a red mark the size of her fingernail. It was not an attractive look, especially on top of her sunburn.

"You have the worst luck lately. Perhaps you should try staying in your room for the remainder of the party."

Could Lord Edwin have made a joke? She smiled. "If only that were possible, my lord. When did you plan to visit your estate?"

"Tomorrow morning. I thought to assemble a small party."

"I am certain Lord Collins will wish to accompany us, and of course, Mother."

He agreed readily enough and added, "I thought you might wish to bring Miss Cannis as well. You seem so close to her."

Her brows drew together. He had never considered including Miss Cannis in their plans before. How unusual. "I will mention it to her, but should we not venture to the dining room?"

Lord Edwin left her as they entered the room, and she went to the large table to find a place to sit.

"Deserted so soon?" Lord Collins asked as he sat beside her.

She shrugged. She had forgotten the sherry in her

hand and took a long sip. She skimmed the crowd but stopped her perusal when she noted Miss Cannis in the very spot Alexa had occupied the previous night. She chatted away in her shy manner with Lord Rudgers, and Lord Rudgers smiled congenially back at her.

"Now what could a marquess find so interesting about a wallflower?" Lord Collins asked at her elbow.

"I believe he holds an exceptional appreciation for music. He even asked her to perform a concert tonight."

"Ah." He reached into his pocket and pulled out the lace fan he had stolen from her in London. He presented it to her and grinned. "For you, my lady."

"I thought I wouldn't get this back until I deserved it." She plucked it from him and placed it on the dinner table. She had missed her fan. Of course, she had plenty of others, but this one was her favorite, mostly because Lord Collins had had it in his possession. Now that he had returned it to her, well, she would keep it tucked away in her room where she could cherish it for the rest of eternity.

"I decided you deserved to have it back now."

She eyed him. She had assumed she would earn her fan back when she ended the relationship with Lord Edwin, not that she would complain now.

It was time for dinner, as evidenced by the pleasant scents wafting through the air, so everyone sat down. "Just look at the way Lord Edwin is staring at his father and Miss Cannis," Lord Collins whispered in her ear.

For the second time that night, Alexa jumped and allowed sherry to escape from its glass. She scowled as another spot appeared on her glove.

"Allow me, my lady." Lord Collins took her hand in his and blotted her glove with his napkin. The candlelight played across his features in a mesmerizing manner, while his hand kept her invigorated. Yes, his attentions pleased her, but she had never thought pleasure would elicit trembling. Both her exterior and interior reacted at his touch, and she could do nothing but stare at him.

He pressed down one final time and drew back, oblivious to the tumultuous reaction he had brought forth. His considerate actions would have no effect on the stain, but she would not point that out to him. Not when she struggled to draw breath.

He straightened and asked, "Is that better now?"

All she could do was nod her response. She hadn't even looked at the bloody thing.

His return smile was so endearing that her heart melted. Truly, how could any woman resist him?

"Do not waste your time looking at Lord Edwin now. His attention has been diverted."

She nodded and drank the rest of her drink. The first course arrived, which allowed Alexa to shake her feelings of desire. She placed her hand firmly in her lap and asked, "You must tell me how Lord Edwin looked at them."

"Let me rephrase that. It is not how he looked at them, more how he looked at her."

When he said nothing else, Alexa simply waited.

"Well"—he leaned in until his lips hovered near her ear—"he looked at her as if he wished to undress her and ravish her right here."

Alexa's hand shot to her fan and began to flick it in an attempt to cool her warm skin. She had to remind herself that he had not said that about her, but about Miss Cannis and Lord Edwin. "My lord! You should not say such things."

His lids lowered as a dangerous glint passed through his eyes. The light from the candles played across his features in a seductive manner as he leaned toward her once more. "One would think the lady who speaks of tupping so easily would also speak of other scandalous matters."

She swallowed, beat her fan once more, and placed it back on the table. She then picked up her fork and eyed her soup. Why couldn't her mind operate in its normal, rational way when around him? Placing her fork in the cream, she scowled as she realized her error.

Lord Collins noted her faux pas, and he smirked at her. "You appear rather distracted tonight, my dear."

She switched utensils, her cheeks heating in embarrassment. Thrusting her spoon into the soup, she scowled and brought it to her lips. "Oh, leave me be and eat your soup."

He sent a long look at her lips, then directed his attention to his own bowl of soup. She ignored his unusual action and turned to the chowder before her.

"Good evening, Miss Farris." A cheery, feminine voice greeted Alexa at her elbow. Lord Collins had captured her attention so well that she hadn't even noticed she sat beside Miss Somers.

"How nice to see you again." Alexa had not seen Miss Somers since her brother's wedding several months prior. "How are wedding preparations proceeding?"

Miss Somers's big, brown eyes shone happily as she gushed, "Oh, it is all simply marvelous. Lord Deering has been so helpful. He really is the most delightful man. Why, just the other day he sent me flowers, and then"—she leaned in with an excited look in her eyes—"he took me for ices at Gunter's!"

"How romantic." Alexa smiled in return, although inwardly, jealousy gnawed at her heart. Lord Edwin had sent her flowers, but only after he angered her at Vauxhall Gardens.

"Yes, Lord Deering is quite the romantic. Of course, he denies it every chance he gets." Miss Somers took a dainty sip of her soup and asked, "How are Lord and Lady Farris?"

Alexa shrugged. "You probably know as well as I. I mostly speak to Gavin through correspondence, and he is not one to write more than necessary."

Miss Somers nodded. "Men can be that way sometimes. I write to Laura weekly, and she writes enough for the both of them."

"They are a good balance, aren't they?"

The silence between them stretched, so Alexa eyed her chowder once more. She had no appetite, so she signaled a footman for a glass of wine. She sipped and closed her eyes, savoring the taste.

"Now is not an appropriate time to nap."

Alexa's eyes flew open as Lord Collins whispered in her ear. She resisted the urge to pick up her fan once more. She did seem to use her fan in excess, but he made her so overheated. "I wasn't about to nap, my lord."

He sat back and looked at her with hooded eyes. "See that you don't. Otherwise, be prepared for my methods of waking you."

The way he had woken her earlier in the day had been lovely, aside from him tickling her nose. She raised an eyebrow in challenge. "If you manage to catch me again, my lord, then go ahead."

A sensuous light filled his eyes, and he smiled. The servants brought in a fruit salad and set the plates before them. Alexa bit into an apple slice and watched him as he did the same. "What happened to your shoulder?"

She exhaled. "I stood beneath a wall sconce."

"Really?"

"Yes." She rolled her eyes. "I think I am cursed here. I cannot seem to avoid disaster."

The servants brought out the next dish and she cringed. "See?" She pointed to the prawn and said, "I hate prawns, yet we are to dine on them every single night."

"Allow me, then." Lord Collins snared one of her prawns and set it on his plate.

"What are you doing?" she asked, her voice rising to a shrill note.

"If you are not going to eat them, then I will." He tore the shell off, and popped it in his mouth. He closed his eyes as he chewed and then peered at her. "Care to share more?"

"That is against all rules of dining etiquette."

He snatched up one more prawn and whispered, "See, no one even noticed."

"That is beside the point."

He placed one of the shells on her plate and grinned. "Now, if Lord Edwin cares to inspect your plate, he will see you have eaten some."

That was surprisingly thoughtful. "Thank you, then."

He inclined his head. "I rather doubt he will notice."

She ducked her head in a blush. She couldn't argue that point, not when he seemed so intent on Miss Cannis and his father. "I can't imagine anyone notices what another eats except those in one's immediate vicinity."

"I would."

"You are much too preoccupied with other people, then."

"I meant I would notice *you*. Not other people."

Oh. She caught herself from saying anything sharp or confrontational. What did he intend, saying ridiculous things to her?

"Can you believe how delicious this fish is?"

Alexa jumped at the unexpected interruption. Miss Somers had spoken, and suddenly, the multitude of other people in the room reappeared. She did not converse with Lord Collins in private, and she had best remember that.

She turned her attention to her plate, only to find her prawns replaced with fish. How had she missed the new course's arrival? She took a bite and agreed, not even taking the time to chew in her rush.

"Too bad Lord Deering had to miss this," Miss Somers said with downcast eyes.

Alexa glanced around and realized that Lord Deering, was, in fact, not in attendance. "Where is he?"

"He had business in London, but he will be here tomorrow. His estate is near to Nettleridge, you know."

"I had not known that."

"Yes. He is very well acquainted with Lord Rudgers." Miss Somers's downcast expression turned cunning as her eyes narrowed.

When Alexa said nothing, Miss Somers said, "Lord

Deering claims Lord Rudgers is a regular boor. He is rude and aloof, unless he approves of you."

Miss Somers always had enjoyed gossip and unsurprisingly knew something interesting about Lord Rudgers. "I wonder if Miss Cannis is one he approves of, then."

Miss Somers looked at the two of them, still deep in conversation, and nodded. "I am sure." She shifted, and the candlelight played off the silvery netting in her brown hair. "Lord Edwin is courting you, yes?"

She could not tell a gossip the truth, so she smiled. "Yes."

"That is what I thought. They say he always tries to please his father. The older brother, however, goes out of his way to irritate Lord Rudgers."

"I hear he is a heavy drinker," Alexa said.

Miss Somers looked at her and laughed. "He is not as bad as all that. Lord Deering is friends with him, you know. The brother, Lord Thornwick, has a horrid reputation, but my dear Lord Deering swears it is partially undeserved."

Servants hurried in with dessert, and Alexa smiled down at a plate of cream puffs. Cream peeked out from the dainty shell, and a light chocolate icing drizzled the top. She would eat every one of them. She bit into one and enjoyed the lightness of the heavenly filling. Instead of closing her eyes as she dearly wished to, she left them open. She did not need to be accused of napping yet again.

"He is as bad as they say."

Alexa turned to eye Lord Collins. "Did you eavesdrop on our conversation?"

"It is not eavesdropping when you are seated right

next to me." As if to emphasize his point, his left foot brushed against hers.

She almost jumped out of her seat from the heat of his leg. She frowned. It wasn't heat. No, the heat approached that of a lightning bolt, or fireworks. Yes, that was it. His touch felt exactly as fireworks must feel, and the fire had not yet faded.

She shook herself. She would not allow the briefest of touches from him to fog her mind anymore. She raised her eyebrow in what she hoped approached a supercilious expression and said, "At least you have something in common with Lord Edwin now. He quite agreed with you in regard to his brother."

His eyes narrowed on her. "Why are you not seated next to Lord Edwin tonight?"

She mumbled her reply, and he asked again. "Well?"

She popped another cream puff in her mouth, chewed, swallowed it, and said, "He doesn't want me to embarrass him again."

He shot her a triumphant grin. He tried to hide it, but failed miserably. "I thought I sensed discord."

She shrugged. "I don't think his father approves of me."

Lord Collins grew serious as he regarded her. "To hell with the whole family."

Two cream puffs remained on her plate, but they had grown tasteless. She set her fork aside and lifted her glass of wine. "Cheers to that, my lord." She then took a drink. That felt good.

A general hush fell over the dining room, and she looked up to see Lord Rudgers standing. "Miss Cannis has agreed to perform for us tonight, so I ask that everyone adjourn to the drawing room. There, you will find tea."

Chapter 15

Alexa took a seat at the back of the room and shuddered as a draft hit her. Lord Collins sat down beside her, and she subsequently forgot the draft as his heat enveloped her. He was very much like a furnace.

The chairs faced a raised platform where Miss Cannis would soon play. Cream and ivory tones adorned the room, from marble floors to Greek columns, and an orange glow streamed through the windows. Lord Collins scanned the crowd, remaining seated until a footman carrying a tray of wine passed by. Then, he jumped up and snagged a couple glasses.

He sat down and whispered in her ear, "He does not waste time, does he?" Lord Collins tipped his glass toward the piano where Miss Cannis had just taken her seat. Beside her stood Lord Edwin, who evidently intended to turn the pages for her.

"No, he does not," she said in response. The evening's ambiance dipped as she realized the truth of the matter. She had wasted an entire season on Lord Edwin, only to find him subpar. She could have used that precious time on finding a worthy suitor, one who would not criticize every aspect of her being.

Lord Collins frowned. She had forgotten to act besotted with Lord Edwin. She could try to remedy her error, but part of her just did not wish to bother anymore.

"I really, really dislike him," Lord Collins said as he turned his attention to the dais.

She raised an eyebrow, and Miss Cannis began to play. The music drowned out Alexa's surroundings, even the enigmatic man besides her. In between sets, she drank her wine and tried to ignore Lord Collins. She could not explain why she ignored him, only that every time she spoke with him, her stomach grew wings. Her frustrating little *tendre* for him did not help matters, either. He remained oblivious to her, even if he did want to kiss her sometimes, and slowly, she grew disheartened.

She lifted her eyes to Miss Cannis and frowned as Lord Edwin turned the page. The two of them made a striking pair. Miss Cannis detested Lord Edwin, but would that change if she grew more familiar with him?

The concert's interlude arrived, and Lord Rudgers declared a pause for a fifteen-minute break.

"Shall we take a stroll, my lady?" Lord Collins asked, dipping his head to hers and offering a slight smile. He reached over, took her empty wine glass from her, and handed it off to a passing footman.

If she remained, she would be forced to watch Lord Edwin drool over Miss Cannis, so she agreed and allowed Lord Collins to lead her out of the drawing room. A door opened to the gravel walkway, and he escorted her outside. The sun still cast enough light to see, but dusk would pass quickly. Even now, a couple of stars sparkled in the sky.

Alexa inhaled a cleansing breath and turned to smile up at him. "There is something about the country air that restores me." She began to walk, and he strolled beside her. "I cannot imagine anything more invigorating."

"You wound me, my lady." His deep voice resonated through her and sent a shiver down her spine.

"I cannot imagine why."

"Most women would not find country air more invigorating than my kisses."

Heat jumped to her cheeks. She could not formulate a response, so she pulled out her fan. His eyes narrowed on the device and he grinned. "Do I need to take that back from you already?"

"Of course not." She snapped her fan shut.

He quirked his brow. "Do you use every fan as enthusiastically, or is this one special?"

"You make it sound as if I beat my fan all the time, when in reality, I only use it around vexing gentlemen."

A shadow flitted over his face. "So there are other gentlemen that irritate you other than myself?"

"No," she said in a shrill tone. Her hand leaped to cover her mouth. "I mean, yes." She scowled. She didn't know how to answer that question, and it aggravated her. Why did he even care if other gentlemen irritated her?

"So, which one is it?"

"No." The truth would have to do. "You are the only gentleman in my acquaintance who irritates me. Are you satisfied now?"

"Hardly." He smirked, but she could not fathom what he alluded to. At her silence, his smirk slipped away. "So, you are not vexed by Lord Edwin?"

"I compared him to warm milk, so you tell me."

"And yet you encourage him."

If he only knew the truth. "I do what I must."

"Which is to throw yourself away needlessly on

one such as Lord Edwin? Surely, you can do better."

She tensed her hands into fists and eyed him. "And then what? Wait for someone that I may compare to *cold* milk?"

He chuckled.

She had taken pride in her response, yet it did nothing but amuse him. "You have your own flaws, so don't think you are above reproach."

"I never said anything to the contrary."

Of course he didn't. He simply pointed out her disastrous match with Lord Edwin, and then acted all witty, and delightful, and vexing.

"Right." She smoothed away a frown and darted a glance at the trees lining the path on which they strolled.

He chuckled, and she turned to regard him. "What is it?"

"Well, if I am the only gentleman who angers you, and Lord Edwin reminds you of warm milk, then I should imagine you would prefer a gentleman like myself."

"You think I would prefer being wed to an irritating fellow? Don't be absurd."

"Is it absurd to prefer a match to someone who can set you aflame?"

Her cheeks heated. That described precisely how she felt around Lord Collins. How had he known? She stubbornly remained silent, and he slowed to a stop, forcing her to join him. "Well? Would you? Or would you prefer a boring life with a gentleman you don't care for?"

"I care for Lord Edwin." Except she didn't. This hole she stood in was much too deep, and her only company in the dank cavern was her lies. She had better draw herself out soon, or else. She shook her head. "No." Her voice emerged small, overshadowed by the darkened sky and whisper of the wind. "I would prefer a match such as you describe."

"You would?" He sounded surprised, and she almost laughed.

"Of course I would. But you are the only gentleman who vexes me, so let's be realistic. I can't very well wed you."

He nodded, but his eyes held shadows. "You are correct. We can never be more than friends."

His words pierced her, and she turned away to hide the pain. Why did she always do this to herself? A small part of her longed for him, but she had never dared dream. Not until he had kissed her. She clenched her hands into tight balls and pressed her nails into the palm of her hands. It hurt, but it was a real pain. One that could allow her to breathe again.

She forced a laugh and said, "Of course. And I would never desire more from you. I don't like you."

His gaze caught and held her, so she forcefully tore her eyes from his and walked along the path. Shadows fell all around her, but she stopped as she caught sight of a soft glow in the foliage. "Do you know why glowworms light up the way they do?"

"To find their mates."

She nodded against the breeze. "I wish humans could shine a light and find their mate. It would make things so much simpler."

"Is this your way of acknowledging your relationship with Lord Edwin is finished?"

Her stupid little lie had ended. She would not live

with it any longer. "Yes. Things between Lord Edwin and myself have...*fizzled*."

"Since when?"

"Since a few days before the house party began."

Silence met her words, so she turned to face him. Shadows masked his face, but the hard line of his mouth told her he did not approve.

"Why then? Why are we here?"

She could not tell him she had wanted to spend time with him. No, the truth would never do. Her heart would shatter into a thousand pieces if she received more rejection tonight. "Lord Edwin promised to invite Miss Cannis's suitor if I came."

"Then where is he?" His voice emerged in a low growl. He was angry with her, but she did not care.

"At sea."

The wind howled amongst the trees that surrounded the path, and the branches overhead swayed. Wisps of her hair flew from her coiffure and surrounded her face, but she cared for nothing other than his reaction.

"Did you know that when you agreed to his deal?"

"Of course not! Believe it or not, I do not relish Lord Edwin's rude remarks or annoying habits. Before I met him, I never worried if I behaved just so, or if my attire was perfect." She scowled as she said the word *perfect* and took a step nearer to him. "I am sick and tired of worrying if my freckles have multiplied, or if the humidity will ruin my hair." She tossed her head back and laughed, a cold, unfeeling laugh. "Despite all that, he still disapproves of me, and the frustrating part is I should not care for his approval."

He moved to her, allowing enough light to

surround him so she could make out his expression. It was angry. Angry and mocking. "The irony in this situation is tragic. You demanded honesty from me after I kissed you, yet you have lied to me in return. I would never have admitted my desire to kiss you otherwise." His lips twisted in a grimace, reinforcing the words he just spoke. He regretted their kiss. It had caused him pain, and she had forced him to recount the event.

She exhaled as guilt assuaged her. "I know. I am a hypocrite."

He nodded. His voice roughened with accusation as he said, "You spoke of your love for Lord Edwin rather convincingly. Am I to understand that you never gave your heart to him?"

"Yes. That would be accurate."

He shifted his weight to his other leg and repeated his previous words, but this time his voice softened as if trying to understand the cipher she presented him with. "You spoke of love so convincingly."

What answer did he require from her? She had spoken of love on occasion and had used her own feelings for Lord Collins to validate her act. She shook her head. She could never tell him the truth, no matter how much a hypocrite that made her. "I am not sure what you want to hear, my lord. Should I profess some grand love for someone? Or continue to claim a nonexistent love for Lord Edwin?"

He growled. "Of course not. I just want to know the truth."

"The truth is you won. Nothing else matters, except I will not marry Lord Edwin." Her noncommittal voice betrayed none of the internal tumult of her emotions.

She swung her gaze to a bench further along the path and walked over to it. She sat, and he joined her there.

There was something comforting in sitting side by side on the bench. He turned to her as the breeze rustled the leaves. "It does not feel like a win. Not like this." He shook his head. His knee brushed hers, and she pulled herself back as if he burned her.

He scowled at her quick retreat, and his voice cooled. "Understand that I expect honesty from you henceforth."

He expected too much. How could she promise something like that when she couldn't maintain honesty with herself, because truthfully, she professed to disliking Lord Collins every chance she found. Could she be honest with him? No.

Her hand twitched to draw out her fan or do anything else to alleviate the tension. He sat immobile next to her with his bright eyes planted on her, awaiting an answer she could not give. So instead, she shook her head. "You demand honesty from me, but for what purpose?" Her voice quieted to a whisper and she said, "Just imagine if I had said I loved you. How would you feel about your precious truth then?"

"I would have been flattered."

"No, you would not." She scowled. She deserved the title of hypocrite, but so did he if he believed his own words. "You would have chalked my feelings up to your supposed irresistible charms and run from me."

"I would never behave in such an abominable way."

Another soft breeze flew through the trees. She did not believe him, but arguing would not benefit either of them. "I guess we will never know, because I dislike you with an astounding intensity."

He laughed, but his laugh held a heaviness that seemed off. "Thank heavens for that."

Alexa leaned her head back against the wood backing on the bench. Several stars sparkled above, and the sky had darkened to a deep blue color. The breeze tore through the trees, and she turned her head to avoid its onslaught. The wind seemed to grow stronger as time progressed tonight. She caught his eyes, and her heart clenched.

"So, friends it is, then." She averted her gaze and waited for his confirmation.

"I—" He abruptly stopped when she looked at him again. He looked hesitant, as if he wanted to say something, but then he shook his head. "Yes," he mumbled, "friends."

Again, the wind blew, and she turned her face to meet it. The breeze cooled her warm skin and allowed the tears that threatened to stay reined in. Lord Collins might not understand what he had just done to her, and she would never let him know the stark truth of it. Her heart lay shattered in the suddenly pained cavity of her chest, and pathetically enough, she wanted him to wrap his arms around her in comfort.

She stood and turned away from him, hiding her face in an attempt to conceal her emotions. "I should return to the manor. If anyone notices my absence, please tell them I have a megrim."

"Of course."

She willed one foot in front of the other toward the house. Music streamed from the open windows, and she turned to go through separate doors further from the drawing room. She hated to miss the concert, seeing as well-played music did not come her way every day, but she could not bear to sit by Lord Collins tonight. Not after he had declared his desire for friendship, yet again.

Maxon swallowed as she disappeared down the path. He hated himself right now, both for his uncaring behavior and for his lack of courage to admit he liked her. A moment had passed where he almost crossed that line. That irreversible line that he should never, ever go down. Because frankly, Alexa was the sort to marry, not engage in a dalliance with.

Several minutes passed in silence until he stood, breaking the silence with the sound of his footsteps trailing back to the manor. She would never wed Lord Edwin, but what about the next gentleman to come along? Would he tolerate that one, or try to chase him off as well? Based on his feelings, he might never part with her, at least with his sanity intact.

He slipped into the crowded room unnoticed and stood by a column in the back. Miss Cannis was in midsong, and the crowd listened to every note. He beckoned over a footman and accepted a glass of wine. He would prefer a stronger beverage, but wine soothed him better than no spirits altogether.

Perhaps he could leave this cursed house party early. No logical reason remained in which to stay, not with Alexa uninterested in Lord Edwin. He drank half his glass and smirked. She had played him nicely on that matter. Until she told him of her disinterest, he had believed she still planned to marry the man, and it had irritated him to distraction. Now, they could part ways until next season.

If he could manage that long.

He drank the rest of his wine. The final note rang out, and Miss Cannis rose. She curtsied, and then hurried off the stage. Lord Rudgers rushed to intercept her and brought her back. He chuckled and said, "She is much too modest, so everyone, please make her feel appreciated for the tremendous job she has done." He kissed her hand and said, "If only we could have her play every night, but alas, she tells me she requires a break tomorrow evening."

Everyone applauded, and Lord Rudgers said, "Now then, tomorrow, there will be an outing to my son's estate. Of course, carriages and horses will be provided, so please assemble at nine at the foyer should you wish to attend."

Another light smattering of applause resounded, and Maxon slipped from the room. He hurried up to his chambers where his scotch and chair awaited him. He had never returned to the library after his run-in with Lord Edwin, but the quiet solitude of his room was more than sufficient.

Maxon entered the room, and Chaney stepped to his side. "Did you have a good evening, my lord?"

Maxon poured himself a couple fingers of scotch and nodded. "It was interesting."

Chaney removed the glass from Maxon's hand and set it down on the side table. Maxon turned around, and the valet divested him of his stiff evening jacket in one smooth gesture. "I see the mystery fan has disappeared."

When Maxon had returned from the ball with Alexa's fan, Chaney had raised an enquiring brow but refrained from asking about it. His nosy valet had enquired numerous times as to why he had a lady's fan, so Maxon had remained silent, just to irritate him.

Maxon accepted his returned scotch and nodded. "Yes, I determined it was the correct time."

"Because sending it to the lady immediately would have been too soon?" Chaney helped to pull off Maxon's snug boots.

"As a matter of fact, yes."

"Hmm."

Maxon took a long sip of his scotch as he observed the nightstand. Alexa's fan had rested there, and every time he beheld it, he had thought of her. Its sudden absence made him feel at a loss somehow, as if something was missing. He sighed and took another drink. The wind still gusted outside, and he could hear the trees rustling even now.

"Ahem." Chaney coughed, and Maxon's eyes flew open. He hadn't even realized his eyes had closed.

His valet indicated Maxon should lean forward so Chaney could remove the stiff cravat. Maxon complied as he considered his scotch and said, "Thank you. That will be all for tonight."

Chaney moved to the large armoire. After several moments with the sound of rustling fabric gracing the room, he shut the oak doors and departed the room without a sound.

The wind howled again, and Maxon cursed. This entire house party was a bloody waste of time. If Alexa had admitted the truth from the start, she could have ended things between herself and Lord Edwin, rather than draw everyone out to this assembly. While he could understand her motives, he could not agree that helping her friend should cause him this much discomfort.

And the worst part of this situation? Maxon liked her. Intensely. But how did that serve him? Instead of a delightful, willing chit, he regularly dealt with a vexing lady who disliked him.

She claimed him as a friend, which should have satisfied his need for her. But it didn't. Why did he detest the thought of her as a friend so? He scowled. Damn this house party, and damn his infernal heart.

Chapter 16

Her dark blue riding habit hugged her in a tight embrace. Every fold fell in its proper place, and every button held precisely where it ought. Her somewhat mismatched hat, securely pinned to her head, completed the outfit. Now, no one could complain about her attire.

The mantel clock suggested she would arrive early, but remaining in her room did little good. When left alone, her mind ended in a preoccupied prison. And the topic of her preoccupation? *Him.* The more time she spent at this house party, the more she grew enamored of Lord Collins. She should not have come to Nettleridge. Her desire to spend time with him only cemented her feelings for him.

Her boot heels clicked as she walked along the uncarpeted hallway. The grand staircase before her curved around the foyer and gave a magnificent view of the entryway. Halfway down the stairs, Lord Edwin materialized, and she groaned. Dressed for riding, he looked extra handsome in his dark brown overcoat. Despite those good looks, she dreaded meeting with him.

"My lady." He smiled as she reached the landing. His smile froze as his gaze alighted on her hat. He brought his eyes back to hers and said, "I hoped I might catch you before the outing today."

He held out his hand, but she did not accept it.

"Why?"

"I thought we might have this conversation alone."

Her eyebrow shot up at his implications, and she shook her head. She would not go off with him alone, because his motive, whatever it was, meant an awkward situation for her. He could say what he needed to say right here and now.

He frowned and shook his head. "You just made this chat so much easier. I don't understand why you have turned into this difficult woman. You used to welcome my presence, but you have changed."

A numb feeling of finality descended on her. Apparently, she would not avoid an awkward situation after all. "Have I?" She might have withdrawn from him, but she had not changed. Had she?

He shook his head once more and leveled a grave stare at her. "I think I will have to withdraw my offer of marriage. Your actions these past few days have been deplorable, and not those of a woman I wish to wed."

Her laugh approached hysterical as she stared at him in disbelief. "Did you fail to hear me every single time I denied your suit? Thank heavens you came to your senses, otherwise I am sure you would never emerge from your delusions."

He sneered at her, baring a set of white teeth. "I didn't want to say this, but you asked for it." The creak of the door overshadowed the sound of his deep inhalation. He did not notice the addition of a third party, only continued to speak a little too loudly. "It has come to my attention that you are a bastard."

Blood rushed to her ears as Lord Collins snarled. He rushed into the foyer and said, "You really should not have said that."

Then, before her very eyes, Lord Collins swung at Lord Edwin. His fist connected with Lord Edwin's nose with a satisfying thud, and Lord Edwin crumpled to the floor in an undignified heap. "I have longed to do that for some time now." Lord Collins smirked and flexed his right hand.

Alexa stood rooted to the floor with her heart beating at a hectic pace. She couldn't take her eyes off Lord Collins, until Lord Edwin stood up. "I don't think you understand the situation," Lord Edwin said with a hand to his nose. "I heard from a certain reputable source that Miss Farris is of questionable lineage. She has deceived me from the start. Now, I have done you a favor by enlightening you as well. No one would want her dubious bloodlines."

Lord Collins surveyed Lord Edwin without an ounce of sympathy. "I wish to pummel you to within an inch of your life. Of course, that would be rather uncouth of me." He smiled and stepped closer to Lord Edwin. "Now, if we did not have an audience..." His voice trailed off, and Lord Edwin blanched. "I suggest you get out of the house before I forget my manners. We will depart at first light tomorrow morning."

"And why not depart now?"

Lord Collins scowled. "We needn't entertain the gossipmongers. If we leave now, people will talk."

Lord Edwin nodded and pulled a pristine white handkerchief from his pocket. He dabbed at his nose. Several small, red stains splotched the handkerchief, and Alexa smiled. Evidently, she was the bloodthirsty sort.

"Very well. But that is all the time I shall grant you. You are no longer welcome in this house." Lord

Edwin turned on his heel, still clutching the handkerchief to his nose, and left.

Lord Collins turned to her with a look of concern on his face. "Are you quite all right? I know that must have been a shock for you."

She nodded. "I am sure I will be fine." Her voice lowered to a whisper. "Thank you, my lord. Your intervention meant more than you will ever know."

"My dear Alexa, the pleasure was all mine."

She wrung her hands as worry set in. "I just wonder who told him. I assumed he already knew of the rumors, but I suppose the knowledge is not as common as I thought." Her mind flew to Miss Somers and she gasped. "You don't think Miss Somers could have?"

He shook his head. "I doubt it. Anyone might have told him. Miss Somers is too pleasant to say something like that to him."

"Yet she is also a gossip." She shivered. "Even a rose has its thorns, my lord."

"You do like to employ your clichés, don't you?"

Her hands dropped to her side, and she stepped to the staircase. "Yes. There is a reason they became cliché."

His demeanor turned serious as he regarded her. "Are you going to be all right?"

She nodded, and he said, "In that case, I think you should run along to your room. I will inform your mother you have a headache."

"Thank you." He bowed low and left. She placed her hand on the rail and began to walk up the stairs when her foot landed on something. Moving aside her skirts, she looked down at a small, silver box. She picked it up and inspected the container. Lord Edwin must have dropped his snuffbox when he fell to the ground. She popped the lid open, took a small amount, and placed it in her handkerchief. She then placed the snuffbox where she had found it and continued on her way.

Lord Edwin had told her ladies did not use snuff, but she would try it anyway. Assuming she could work up her nerve.

****

Alexa had napped. She could not seem to help herself, not when she considered her travels the next day. She would rest then as well, but not with the same ease as now, due to the rollicking of the carriage.

She still felt groggy, but something had woken her from her slumber. She rubbed her eyes as a knock sounded on the door. She called out to the person to enter, curious who would visit her now.

Miss Cannis rushed in, and Alexa bolted upright. "Whatever is the matter?"

Tears streamed down Miss Cannis's face, and her pretty brown eyes looked red and puffy. She flew to the bed and sat down in a graceless heap. "Oh, Miss Farris, the very worst thing has happened."

"Well?" Alexa prompted. She had never seen Miss Cannis behave this way, not even at the countless balls where she received no offer to dance.

She pulled a soggy white handkerchief from her pocket and dabbed her eyes. Alexa stood and found a different handkerchief and tossed it at her. Then, she sat on the bed and leaned toward her friend, eager to hear the cause of her distress.

"We were all at the house party, and I happened upon the music room." Her eyes went to Alexa's, and she smiled through her tears. "Did you know Lord Edwin has a music room? It is quite the most beautiful room I have ever seen. There is white crown molding and minty green walls."

Alexa coughed. Miss Cannis was getting sidetracked.

"Yes, well, Lord Edwin found me there, and we began to discuss music." She dabbed her eyes once more, wiping away the remnants of her tears. "I had not realized he enjoyed music so, and then he told me I was beautiful." She blushed and closed her eyes. "He smelled so nice, and he was so kind. He asked me if I would consider playing a song for him. I agreed, and I played the piece he chose."

Her eyes reopened, and she shook her head. She appeared transfixed on the window, and then she rushed on to say, "At the end of the song, he leaned down and kissed me. It all seemed so romantic, and I even kissed him back. He moved to sit by me on the piano bench and placed his arms around me. I should have stopped—" She hesitated and then shuddered. "—but I didn't, and then the doors to the music room burst open and Miss Somers came in with some other ladies." Her eyes went to Alexa's and she whispered, "I am ruined, Miss Farris. Ruined."

Alexa sat immobile. How could this have happened? Lord Edwin could not have moved on already, but then, he had devoted an unusual amount of attention to Miss Cannis lately. She frowned. Miss Cannis disliked Lord Edwin. Strongly.

Miss Cannis coughed and said, "I am so very sorry, Miss Farris. He was yours, and I did the unthinkable to my best friend." Tears welled up once more, and several large drops spilled down her cheeks.

"Did you just apologize to me?" If anything, she should apologize to Miss Cannis for letting Lord Edwin loose on her.

The pain in the depths of her friend's eyes almost broke Alexa's heart. "Of course. I had no right to kiss Lord Edwin. I understand if you hate me now."

Alexa laughed in disbelief. "I could never hate you, and there is no need for you to apologize." She laid her hand over Miss Cannis's and whispered, "I am so sorry this has happened to you. I know how much you wanted something special. Someone like your captain."

Miss Cannis shook her head. "Lord Edwin has promised to marry me." She heaved a sigh and offered a brave smile. "Lord Rudgers looked elated that we are to marry. Mother, also, is excited."

"That is all well and good, but you want to marry for love."

She nodded and dabbed at her eyes. "I never truly believed I would get that chance. Mother tells me this is the best thing that could have happened to me, and I am sure she is right."

In terms of wealth and status, Lord Edwin was much better than Victoria could hope for. "You don't like Lord Edwin, though."

She shrugged and shifted so her other hand propped her up on the bed. "I don't have much of a choice now, do I?"

Alexa nodded, despite her reservations. Miss Cannis's circumstances allowed for precious few options seeing as her parents would not want a ruined spinster on their hands. She could not even find respectable work as a governess at this point. At least

Lord Edwin had done the honorable thing and offered to marry her.

The bed creaked as Alexa stood. She needed to act as a bulwark for her friend. She crossed to the window and turned around with a smile. "You will preside as the mistress of the house you just toured. That impressive music room will be yours."

Miss Cannis rose and nodded. "There are quite a few good things that I should be grateful for. In time, I imagine I will appreciate my circumstances more. I just have to get to know Lord Edwin and hope for the best."

"He really is not such a bad man." Alexa did not condone lying through one's teeth, but this situation warranted it.

Miss Cannis gave her a dubious smile. "We leave in the morning for London. I have to assemble my trousseau. You will write to me? Please?"

"Of course."

Miss Cannis hugged her and then left as swiftly as she arrived. Alexa wrapped her arms around herself in a tight hold as the door shut. What a momentous day this had been, and it had not reached its end. She turned back to regard the overcast sky and sighed.

She held such mixed emotions for Miss Cannis's predicament. While her friend's life would be one of a respectable, wealthy lady, she would endure it with an ass. Granted, Lord Edwin might treat her well so long as his father approved of her. Alexa could not imagine Miss Cannis behaving in an untoward manner, so it might go very well for her.

Her spirits hung low, what with the news of such scandal in relation to her best friend and her previous suitor. She had caused her friend's inveiglement with a scoundrel. And she could do little but wish her friend well.

She walked over and pulled the bellpull. With all of today's excitement, she would remain in her room for the remainder of the day. She did, after all, have the perfect excuse of a headache.

****

Lady Farris had shown concern over Alexa's megrim but still chose to go on the outing to Lord Edwin's estate. Maxon had then informed her of their departure in the morning. He had used business as an excuse, and she had been very understanding.

He considered going on the excursion but nixed that idea in favor of anything else. If Alexa was not present, there would be very little enjoyment. He went up to his room, where Chaney helped him from his riding clothes and into more appropriate attire. Then he checked his pocket watch. He could read a book or perhaps take a stroll. The overcast sky promised rain, so he settled in to read a book.

He must have dozed off, because he abruptly discovered his book lying on the floor and voices echoing outside his door. He shook his head and stood. Alexa's penchant for naps must have rubbed off on him. He had never taken naps, and now, he had engaged in two.

He swung his door open and walked down the hall.

"Lord Collins!"

He turned around to find Lord Deering with Miss Somers at his side.

"Lord Collins, how nice to see you!" Lord Deering smiled as he drew near. "Would you care to join us for a drink? I am certain Miss Somers would willingly partake of some sherry as well."

She offered a demure smile in agreement, and Maxon nodded. They walked the rest of the way to the library in silence.

"Did you hear the news, my lord?" Miss Somers asked as excitement tinged her face.

"I do not believe I have."

Her grin broadened, and she poured herself a glass of sherry. "Lord Edwin has compromised Miss Cannis. I saw it with my own two eyes. He had his arms around her in a torrid embrace, kissing her as if his life depended on it."

The decanter he held almost slipped from his hand. He put the stopper back on and tried his best to hide the shock in his voice. "Is that right?"

"Oh yes! Lord Edwin, bless his heart, has offered to marry Miss Cannis, and she said yes." Her voice lowered, and she leaned forward in her excitement. "Not that she was in a position to say anything other than yes. She is so very poor." She tittered, but when he did not look amused, stopped. Her eyes narrowed and she asked, "How do you imagine Miss Farris will react?"

"Why on earth would Miss Farris care?" Lord Deering asked as he leaned against the yellow wall.

"Well, dear, Miss Farris and Lord Edwin were a thing before her best friend snatched him away."

"Ah. That is awkward."

She tittered again and returned her gaze to Maxon. "I wonder if she has heard yet."

Maxon scowled and downed his drink. "I am sure I do not know, madam." He nodded to Lord Deering and hastened from the library. The bloody room was cursed, and he would not return to it if he had any say in the matter.

He stopped himself as he walked. His feet had a mind of their own, directing him to Miss Farris's room. He turned around and went to his room instead.

"I think I shall go riding," he called out to Chaney as the door closed behind him.

Chaney halted folding a pair of breeches intended for a portmanteau and nodded. He turned to the wardrobe and pulled out the necessary items. "This is a bit late for one of your rides, my lord."

"Yes, but I need to occupy myself. Perhaps I will ride to the village for supper." And lots and lots of ale.

"Very good, my lord."

Chaney helped him change, and then Maxon left. He would avoid people as much as possible because he could not stomach gossiping about Alexa. No one stopped him on his way down, or at the stables where he waited for the groom to saddle Tyr. The ride to the village did not take long, and soon he settled on a tavern on the outskirts of the little town.

He sat at an unoccupied table next to a window and signaled the barkeep. The man brought over a tankard of ale, and he ordered sustenance. A dark-haired serving girl carried a hearty beef stew to him, and he smiled at her. He handed her a shilling and said, "If you ensure I do not run out of ale, there will be much more for you."

An eager light entered her eyes, and she curtsied. "Of course, my lord."

He then proceeded to eat. He did not taste any of his stew, only chewed and swallowed. How could he enjoy the meal when Alexa preoccupied his thoughts so? This disturbing business of Lord Edwin's compromising Miss Cannis should not have surprised him, not after considering Lord Edwin's actions. Why, he should have expected it. Lord Edwin always searched for his father's approval, and his father had made it evident that he approved of Miss Cannis.

Now, the question remained, how had Alexa reacted to the news? Was she upset, or did she not care? Lord Edwin had courted her for most of the season, so she must have experienced some sort of emotion. Maybe she was, even now, crying in her room. Would anyone comfort her, or was the very person she normally received comfort from the one who would now marry her ex-suitor? He shuddered at the thought. Alexa hung in a difficult position, assuming she cared, or even knew of the day's events.

He finished his stew and downed his pint. Therein lay the crux of the matter. He had no idea if she did care that Lord Edwin had ruined her best friend. He picked up the full pint that had appeared in front of him and took a swig. Matters should never have reached this point. If Alexa had listened to him in the first place, they would never have attended this house party and no one would have been compromised.

The light of the sun shifted as he sat there, lost in thought and in his cups. He couldn't remain here any longer, not with so many unknowns weighing on him. He stood and swayed. The serving girl rushed to his side, and he eyed her. A pair of firm, lush mounds peeked out from her bodice, but they did not even make him look twice. Instead, he paid his tab, gave her a ludicrous tip, and left. He really had overtipped her, but at least one person ought to feel in good spirits tonight.

He rode to the manor and left his horse with a groom. He took each step with the intention of going to his room, but he knew deep within his heart he would go to her. He had to check on her. The supper time drew near, but everyone would depart in the morning. No house party would continue after such a scandal.

He knocked on her door and entered without waiting for her to speak. He closed the door behind him and stopped. She sat on the floor facing the window with the soft light of dusk around her. She turned her head to him and smiled. Her hair fell down her back, and she wore her nightgown. He couldn't think. Not when she rested in such an alluring fashion, framed by the lingering light of the waning day.

Chapter 17

"My lord, how good of you to join us." She smiled at him and patted the spot next to her. "Do sit."

He looked around the sparsely furnished room. The dark green color of her room made the room look smaller, cozier. "Who is 'us'?"

"Why, Riesling and myself, of course." She smiled, and he eyed the bottle next to her. How she had managed to procure an entire bottle was beyond him.

She lifted the wine and took a drink. His mind was addled, but even he could see it was inadvisable to approach her, or even remain with her in the room. He should go, but he ignored that thought and sat down.

"How are you doing, Alexa?" He searched her face and discovered nothing to confirm or deny her grief. Her eyes shone bright from the drink, but aside from that, he could identify no obvious change.

"Whatever do you mean, my lord? Or are you hinting about the little scandal that happened today?" She sighed and traced the rim of her wine bottle with her index finger. "I cannot imagine why that should bother me."

He scowled. "I do not care that you did not love him, and you claim no desire to wed the man, but that doesn't mean you should be without feeling."

She shook her head. Her hair shifted around her, and he had to hold himself back from touching it. Or partaking of its delectable rose scent. "I wasted so much time on him." Her lips twisted into a small, sad smile. "We females only get a few years to marry before we are considered on the shelf and unmarriageable." She sighed and took another swig of wine. A small amount ran down her chin, and his breath caught as he considered licking the wine from her skin. "In a way, I suppose I should be grateful to him. He is to marry Miss Cannis, and I feared she would never find anyone."

"So you are not anguished, then?" he asked as he eyed her profile. She was exquisite, with her hair draped over one shoulder and her small bare feet sticking out of her nightgown.

"No." She shook her head, and the pain in her eyes struck him. "But this disastrous union is my fault. She should not be with a gentleman, no matter his status, unless she likes him."

"I fear that is not how the world works, and this is not your fault. She was in the room with him on her own volition. You did not force her to be there."

"Yet if I hadn't begged an invitation for her, she wouldn't have attended at all. Lord Edwin would barely have registered her existence."

"You can only be held accountable for the wrongdoings you commit. Not for the consequences of your innocent actions."

Something in her eyes changed, and her eyes flashed with deviltry. "Oh? I have often blamed you for your own innocent actions."

He leaned forward with interest. "Do tell."

"When I was a little girl, I imagined myself in love with you."

His heart thumped in painful acknowledgement. "How was that my fault?"

She broke eye contact with him and began tracing the lip of the bottle as she said, "You were pleasant to me. You considered my feelings and strove to include me when Gavin would not. So, even though you had innocent intentions, when you broke my heart, I blamed you."

"Is that why you dislike me? You hold a grudge for an act I never knew I committed?"

She smiled, her finger continuing in its entrancing motion. "Yes, and no."

She was much too complicated to decipher, but one thing remained clear. She still preferred friendship with him. And that knowledge pulled on him like the heaviest of weights. But what should he do? Leave? He couldn't do that to her, not when she remained in such a fragile state.

"Those two situations are different."

"How so?" She leveled a stare at him and raised a brow, her finger pausing on the rim of the bottle.

"You never could have foreseen what would come of this house party, while I should have known better."

"Oh no. I should have known what Lord Edwin's plans were. All he cared about was pleasing his father, and then, his father approved of Miss Cannis."

"And yet, it was not possible, just as it was not possible for me to know you held a schoolgirl crush on me." He sighed. "Listen, you did nothing wrong. Nothing."

Slowly, she nodded and resumed her circular motions on the bottle. "I thought you had known of my crush. Otherwise, why did you stop visiting?" She swung her gaze to his, without masking a haunted expression in their bluish gray depths. Her eyes darted away, and she rushed to say, "I know you had other reasons to stay away, but Gavin went with you. I missed him."

"Neither of us should have stopped visiting. The Farris clan was the closest thing I had to a family of my own." His voice lowered. "You know, after my father passed. No one else cared for me."

Her eyes grew round at his words. "I had not realized that, my lord. How sad."

He shrugged and stretched out his legs before him. "I have some distant relations, but aside from that, your family was, well, my family."

Her lips parted, and his eyes settled on them. His mind clouded over, but he shook it clear and looked away. "That is the reason I visited so often as a child. My relatives did not want me, but you seemed to."

"Yes," she whispered. "I do." She blushed and turned from him, but he could still see the rosy glow on her cheek.

"What do you mean by that?" he asked a little too roughly. His breath caught as she turned to regard him with those large, expressive eyes. He needed to know the answer. Needed to know if she had simply misspoken, or if she still disliked him as she so oft claimed. She couldn't, could she? Could one feel a strong sense of love for someone who did not return the emotion? Of course one could.

She ignored him and stood, swayed precariously, and then went to the bed where her reticule lay. Her dark hair ended in a flurry of curls at her lower back. If she joined him in bed, would her hair encompass him?

She returned to her seat and placed her reticule on the floor beside the bottle of wine. She pulled out a handkerchief and spread it out before her on the floor. "Have you ever tried snuff, my lord?"

"Yes," he said, leaning over to identify the small mound in the center of her handkerchief. How had she managed to procure snuff? She was a very resourceful girl. He eyed her wine bottle and snatched it up. He took a swig and returned the bottle to her. He required some wine if he had to speak with her about snuff of all things.

"I wish to try it."

He exhaled. Her countenance exuded mischief, and it drew him to her like a moth to a flame. "Do you need help, or do you know what you are doing?"

"You would help me? Lord Edwin said snuff was not for women."

Maxon shook his head. Lord Edwin was exasperating, to put it mildly. "Plenty of women use snuff. It is extremely popular."

Her brows drew together in confusion. "Then why have I never seen any women use it?"

"I can only surmise your mother did not want you to know of it, so you never learned of its existence." He grinned. "I am just surprised you didn't run across someone using it at a ball."

"Lord Edwin did."

She sounded defensive, and he laughed again. "I wonder how many times he used it around you before you noticed."

She scowled and lifted her bottle of wine. She took one final drink and said, "It is now or never. I must try this before I lose my nerve."

"Of course, my lady." He leaned over to the handkerchief and picked up a pinch. "Take a small amount between your fingers like this." He placed an appropriate measure between his thumb and index finger and showed her. "Now, place it up to your nose and inhale. *Gently*."

She did as instructed and brought the snuff to her nose. Then, she inhaled and erupted in a bout of sneezing. In between sneezes, she said, "This cannot be normal. It burns." Her eyes watered, and he chuckled. He could have warned her that might happen, but this was much more entertaining.

Her sneezes stopped, and she placed a hand on her forehead. "Is it supposed to make my head feel fuzzy?"

Again, he laughed. "Yes. That is the nicotine in the snuff."

"Well, I cannot say I approve."

"Most people use snuff for that exact reaction." He reached into his pocket and pulled out his handkerchief. "Here. Blow into this, and it should clear your nose."

She used the square cloth daintily and then groaned. "You know, I do not think it was wise to mix snuff with spirits."

"Are you feeling nauseated, dearest?" His breath caught at the familiar term, but she did not seem to notice.

She nodded, so he pulled her to him and leaned her against him. There was no conceivable way he would be able to sit this way for long, so he lifted her and scooted them back until he leaned against the bed. Then, he nestled her in the crook of his arm and used his other hand to repetitively smooth back her hair. Her body against his, however innocent, felt so right. He would give up a peaceful night to spend the remainder of the evening just like this, with her clothed and asleep against him.

She relaxed and said, "It is unwise of you to be in my room, my lord."

"Maxon," he ordered.

"Maxon." She tested his name, and he smiled. He liked the way she said his name. "How did you come by the name Maxon? It is rather unusual."

"It was some great-great-great-grandmother's surname." He smoothed back her hair again, and the scent of roses surrounded him. He inhaled and resisted the urge to nuzzle her, any part of her. "What about you? Alexa is hardly a typical name."

She laughed, but he could tell she neared sleep. "It is short for Alexandra."

"I see." He looked down at the length of her and couldn't help but appreciate the way her skirt had risen to expose her left calf. It looked shapely, and inviting, and honor dictated he not do a damned thing about it.

"Will you return to London tomorrow?"

"I don't believe so. I think I shall go home." After all, he had a new woman to get over. How had he developed feelings for two ladies in such a short time period? While inconceivable, here he lingered, losing his heart more and more with every moment she rested in his arms.

"We shall go to the countryside. Someone must oversee the gardens." She shifted against him, her voice dropping to a sleepy whisper. "It is all my fault, you know."

"What is?"

"Miss Cannis would never have been forced to

marry Lord Edwin if I hadn't been involved in the whole mess. Her unhappiness is my fault."

He placed a gentle kiss on the top of her head, wishing beyond measure that he could lessen her pain. "It is not your fault."

"It is. And now I shall return home. You won't be there, no matter how much I wish…" The last remnants of her whisper receded, and she fell fast asleep.

His heart constricted.

That whisper dealt the final blow to his being, and now he knew, without a shadow of a doubt, he loved her.

He loved her.

Shutting his eyes, he savored the feel of her against him. She burrowed her head a little deeper into his shoulder, and he resisted the urge to awaken her and tell her. Such a foolhardy desire could not come to fruition.

No. It was best if he left and saved himself the embarrassment of confessing his feelings.

So, he inhaled her scent, and then picked her up to carry her to the bed. He laid her down and pulled the coverlet over her. Taking a moment to gaze down on her uninterrupted, he wished he could deny all logic and just stay with her. Forever. She was beyond beautiful, more beautiful than any of the roses she loved so. Both inside and out.

He bent over and placed one final soft kiss on her lips. He should not have ventured to her room so early in the night, but then he would have missed this time with her.

Hell, maybe Lord Edwin had the right of it. Wed her by whatever means necessary.

****

Her maid woke her before the sun had a chance to, and Alexa prepared for the ride ahead without a single vocal complaint. Her head hurt, and her nose felt a bit off, but worse than that, she could remember every single word she said to Lord Collins, and it was mortifying. Especially when she said she wanted him. Nothing would allow her to forget that foolish declaration.

Her maid helped her into her travel dress, and she lay back down on the bed. "Let me know when we shall depart."

"They are all waiting for you now, my lady."

Alexa growled and pushed herself back to standing. She hurried down to the carriage where her mother stood. Unsurprisingly, Lord Collins did not meet her to say goodbye. After last night, he had best stay far, far away.

A footman helped her into the carriage, and she reclined against the bench. She would nap all the way to Wiltshire, where she would say hello to Gavin and Laura, and then sleep off the exertions of her travels.

"Are you unwell, Alexa? Have you not recovered from your headache?" her mother asked as she climbed into the carriage.

"I am fine." Alexa peered at her mother and offered a reassuring smile. "I am just experiencing my monthlies."

"Well, that does not make for an enjoyable travel day. If you require anything, let me know." Her mother pulled out a novel and settled in to read.

Alexa closed her eyes and attempted sleep. The carriage rocked forward, and they began their tedious journey. The sway of the conveyance lulled her, and she soon fell fast asleep.

She woke to find her mother's hand on her shoulder. "Do you wish to stop for luncheon?"

Shaking her head, she opened her eyes and sat up. "That won't be necessary." She never had an appetite when travelling.

"Very good." Lady Farris's forehead creased as she looked at Alexa. "We haven't discussed what happened yet." Alexa's heart clenched. How could her mother know of last night? No one knew except for her and Lord Collins.

"How are you now that Lord Edwin is to marry Miss Cannis?" Alexa almost laughed out loud at the relief which followed her mother's question. How could she have forgotten such a monumental event?

Alexa waved her hand and turned to the window, affecting indifference. Trees flew by as they slowly made their way through the countryside. "I am fine, Mother." She laughed and hoped that would help allay her mother's fears. "If anything, I feel sorry for Miss Cannis. She detests Lord Edwin."

Her mother relaxed and gave a slight nod. "Mrs. Cannis is beyond excited by the circumstances, but I could not even countenance the idea of congratulating her when I didn't know how you felt."

"Well, you shall have to write her a letter to express your felicitations."

"She thought we might like to attend the wedding."

Alexa would give up gardening for a month to attend Miss Cannis's wedding. Her eyes misted at the thought that she could never visit Miss Cannis, not so long as Lord Edwin held a grudge. Knowing him, that grudge could linger indefinitely. She cleared her throat and said, "I fear that will not be possible."

"Oh?" Her mother raised an eyebrow, and Alexa informed her of some of the events of the past few days.

When Alexa reached the part where Lord Edwin accused her of her illegitimacy, her mother inhaled and her face turned ashen. "Don't worry, Mother. Lord Collins knocked some respect into him, quite literally. As a result, I do not believe we will be welcomed at the wedding."

"You never have asked me if the rumor is true." Her mother turned her gaze to the window, but not before betraying a twinge of sorrow.

"That is because I do not want to know. I have my family, and the rumor's validity changes nothing."

Her mother continued to gaze out the window but turned enough to give the ghost of a smile. Alexa laid her head back down and closed her eyes. Occasionally, she wondered if the rumor held merit, but she had determined long ago that it did not matter. She sighed and let her mind drift. They would reach Wiltshire, and then she could immerse herself in mind-numbing gardening.

Chapter 18

A week flew by in tedious boredom for Maxon, accompanied by an unusual feeling of lethargy that refused to leave him. He continued with his normal activities, such as his early morning ride, meals, and estate business, but something was missing. He did not want to think about the missing part of him, but nothing could quite get him to stop.

Heartbreak had beaten him down before, but this puncture to his heart felt different from the betrayal he had faced earlier in the season. When the duchess had tried to ruin Alexa, his feelings for her had shattered, replaced with bitterness. Alexa's absence felt as though he had pieced together a puzzle, except for the very last piece. That last piece, whether her denial or affirmation, would finish the puzzle.

He rounded a bend in his extensive gardens and his gaze settled on a luscious red rose. Of course he should happen upon the one thing that reminded him most of her. He leaned down and sniffed the rose and, immediately, felt as if she stood there with him.

Her memory had haunted him for the past week. He needed to know the truth: did she harbor any real feelings for him or not? He knew of his own feelings for her. He loved her. Most ardently. Of course, she might not return his feelings, but could he allow himself to stand idly by and not find out?

He shook his head and entered his home. The servants had taken to avoiding him, which was a definite difference to how they behaved before the house party. While not grouchy, he did emit an unapproachable air, and he liked it that way.

He entered his chambers, and Chaney emerged from the closet. "My lord." He offered a stiff bow and asked, "How may I be of assistance?" Even Chaney behaved a touch more aloofly.

"I would like to change."

Chaney nodded but surprised Maxon by asking, "Don't you normally depart for Wiltshire this time of year?"

Maxon shot him a glare, but Chaney ignored it and raised a scornful brow. "With all due respect, my lord, your household would appreciate a break from your gloomy frown."

"I have only been here a week."

"Precisely, my lord."

Again, Maxon glared at him. Every other year, Gavin had invited him to visit at the end of the season so they could attend a nearby horse race, but Gavin had expressly written him this year to cancel their plans.

"I cannot have behaved worse than I did a few months ago."

"Can't you?" Chaney asked as he helped Maxon disrobe.

Maxon turned to his valet with a scowl. "What are you saying?"

"While no one in the house would ever complain, my lord, there might have been a few comments about your dark mood. I simply think a diversion might help lighten said mood."

Turning toward his wall of windows, Maxon took a few steps to look out on his estate. A large lake filled most of the window, and several gardens stretched out before his eyes. Alexa had never visited his home, but every part of it told him she would love it. Although, one would hope she would avoid falling. She had come too near to taking a dip in the pond at Nettleridge, and his deep lake would not do for a lady to take a casual swim.

He smiled and turned back to Chaney.

"Help me back into my jacket, and pack enough to last me at least a week." He scowled. "No, make it a fortnight. We leave within the hour." The ride to Wiltshire would take little more than an hour. Maxon would have to deny his receipt of Gavin's letter, which made for the perfect excuse to see *her*.

And then, he could win her. No matter what it took, he would wed his lady.

****

The hot glare of the sun pounded on her back, but Alexa paid it no mind. She was too busy hacking away at the myriad of weeds in the herb garden. One dandelion in particular seemed to beckon to her, and she placed a hand at its base with every intention of eliminating it from her garden. The dratted thing had grown much too large, and when she pulled, it did not budge.

As much as large weeds frustrated her, they could not compare to the insurmountable feelings of longing she held toward Maxon. "*Maxon*." She tested his name on her lips for the first time since that night and frowned. Pulling herself to a crouched position, she put all her strength into pulling at the weed, and this time, it pulled loose with a loud plopping sound.

That sound did wonders for her soul, just as the ones the past few days had. In fact, every single weed she did away with reinforced her notion that she would flourish better in her current predicament. Alone, without suitors.

"Oh, Tessa, can you believe *he* is here?"

Alexa's head reared up as the passing laundry maids walked by.

"Is he as handsome as ever?" the other woman asked.

"Of course, although I swear he looks even more tasty. Those blue eyes…"

The voices faded from hearing, and Alexa frowned. Of whom did they speak? She latched onto a thistle and yanked it out in one swift tug. She surveyed the thistle with a victorious smile. She had managed to pull the entire root, which was no small feat. Throwing it behind her, she turned to inspect her work. A steady stream of vanquished foes littered the ground in her wake, leaving a clean herb garden next to the mess of weeds.

Her brother had lapsed in his supervision of the gardens and ought to feel ashamed of himself. Her task had appeared quite intimidating when she first started. Now, however, she had run out of work, except for the herb garden, and she did not know what she would do when she finished her work here.

Of course, she knew what she would do. She would sit in her room and wallow in self-pity that her love did not return her feelings.

Maybe with absence, he would realize he missed her. After all, they said absence made the heart grow fonder, and her heart had grown fonder and fonder of Maxon since she left the house party. No, that didn't sound quite right. Rather, her heart brimmed with love for him, and in a few more days, it would overflow. When that happened, she would find herself in a sodden mess on the floor. She would have to chalk the emotional outburst up to another monthly course, and hopefully her mother would not grow suspicious.

The basil had multiplied to a miniforest. She moved to pull an offensive weed from its midst but stopped as she nearly ran into a garden spider. She jumped up and screeched. This was why she kept footmen handy.

She scanned the surrounding area for a servant, but no one came. The sun bore down extra hot that morning, but if she could handle the heat, then the footmen should also. She couldn't very well move a spider on her own, so she hitched up her skirts and marched around the corner of the house. She would find someone to aid her.

As she rounded the corner, she ran straight into a brick wall, except it wasn't a brick wall. It was a man. His hands stopped her from falling, and he said in a polite tone, "Excuse me. I did not see you there."

She stilled at the familiar voice. Her wide-brimmed hat shielded her from his view. She wore simple clothing which must appear servant-like. She murmured an apology and began to walk around him, but his hand caught her arm in a firm grip.

"Alexa?" he asked in surprise as he plucked the hat from her head.

She gasped and reached for her hat. He smirked and held it up high, well past his smug, handsome face.

"Give me that."

He held it even higher, but she stopped as she remembered herself. She brought her hands to her side and tried to contain her anger. "What are you doing here?"

"I ventured out for a ride and thought to drop by." He sounded serious, but he had not made a habit of dropping by uninvited in the past.

"Oh? Just to say hello?" She brushed aside a tendril of hair and scowled. She must look a fright, with dirt caking her fingernails and possibly even threaded in her hair.

"More or less. I came to attend the Almhurst race with your brother."

"I can't imagine Gavin would leave Laura for so long a time."

"That is what I am told." He shrugged as his eyes roamed over her person. "When is the last time you bathed?"

"I beg your pardon?" she asked, swinging her gaze to his. She did not care how attractive he looked with a light sheen of sweat on his brow. The noon air felt smothering, and she doubted he smelled much better than she. "You are hardly one to talk. When did you arrive?"

"About thirty minutes ago."

"Shouldn't you be in your rooms, then? You could benefit from a thorough cleansing as well."

"My, aren't we feisty this morning?" He grinned at her. He lowered her hat in steady increments, and she took that moment to snatch it from his grasp.

She thrust the serviceable hat back on her head and turned away from him. The herb garden lay around the corner, and she could feel him follow her as she made her way back. As she reached her previous location, she turned to him and smiled. "You might as well make yourself useful and remove this obstruction from my path." She pointed to the spider and waited for him to step over and either kill the creature, or somehow extricate it.

He peered over her shoulder. His nearness unnerved her, so she held her breath in hopes that he would not notice. "What am I removing?"

Pointing once more at the spider, she raised her eyebrow when his gaze did not follow her direction. Instead, he looked down on her and grinned. "You know, you look good dirty."

She could not hold her breath any longer, so she exhaled and drew in a deep, invigorating breath. His very masculine scent hit her, and if the spider had not been in her way, she would have backed up. If she had been capable of movement, that is. The very fact that he complimented her made her knees grow weak, just as it made her heart swell.

Her brow rose, and she considered his statement. It struck her as unusual, at best, no matter how endearing. "Thank you, my lord. I can't say I've heard that particular compliment before."

"I cannot imagine why," he said as he stepped past her. He knelt next to the spider, picked it up, and moved it to a different part of the garden.

Her cheeks heated at his compliment, and she knelt by the basil once more. "Thank you for moving the spider, my lord. The footmen all quail when I ask them."

He moved to stand and looked down on her with a

face devoid of emotion. "There are no poisonous spiders here, so I cannot imagine why, but then, you didn't exactly move it yourself. Why is that?"

"I don't like to touch the creature. Garden spiders are useful, but I prefer not to deal with them." She peered up at him from beneath her hat brim. "Well, don't just stand there. Either help or go away." She longed to be in his presence, but he should leave. Immediately.

He knelt beside her on the unearthed soil and grinned. "Did you miss me so much that you would choose to share your favorite pastime with me? How delightful."

She pulled at a thistle and snapped the plant off at the point the stem reached the dirt. She began to dig around the root to gain a handhold and said, "I hadn't even noticed your absence."

He leaned over to her under the pretext of pulling a weed, and Alexa focused on the ground before her. She would not notice the way his minty scent mingled with sweat and horses as it surrounded her, and she would definitely not notice the way his body almost touched hers. Instead, she grabbed the root with all her might and pulled hard. She felt the root give, but she did not react quickly enough. Her behind hit the soft ground with a thud. It was one of her least ladylike moments, and it just had to be with *him* looking on.

He turned and surveyed her. "Do you fall often, or just when I am around?"

She crossed her arms and refused to answer. If she said yes, it would make her appear clumsy, but if she said she fell only around him, it would sound much too flirtatious. "Well, are you going to help me up?"

"I would love to, my lady." He extended his hand, and she regretted her entreaty the second their skin touched. Tingles raced up her arm, but as usual, he appeared oblivious.

He pulled her to him, and she regained her crouched position. "Thank you, my lord." She began to brush off her bottom, until he smirked at her. He did not say anything, which forced her to ask, "What?"

"Why is it, long ago, you pointed out the lack of compliments I gave you, yet you never give me one?"

His question floored her, and she paused to consider him. "Gentlemen do not require compliments." Especially gentlemen such as him.

He turned to the bed of basil and began to pull at one of the plants.

"My lord."

He swung his head back and waited.

"That is not a weed." He removed his hand and she said, "Maybe it is best you don't help, after all."

He nodded, but his eyes remained on her. "Now you tell me I am a poor gardener. Is there anything I do well, Alexandra?"

The way he said her name forced her to take a moment to draw breath. "You obviously know there are many things you do well."

"Then name one."

She would never get any gardening done with him around, so she stood. He rushed to join her in standing, and she stepped around him. Every compliment she could think of would sound much too coquettish to state, so her rational mind told her to leave.

He caught her arm as she attempted her escape. "Well, name something." A cunning grin spread across his face as his voice turned husky. "For example, I mentioned earlier that you look good dirty."

She scowled at him and tried to shake his arm off her. He would not budge. "Fine." Warning bells blared in her mind, but she ignored them as she stepped nearer to him. "You look far better clean." Then, she brought her hand to his face and smeared dirt on him starting at his temple and ending at the tip of his chin. The wide swath of mud contrasted with his light coloring, and she grinned.

He caught her hand as it fell from him, and his blue eyes narrowed on her. "That was possibly the best compliment you could give me." His arm went around her and he pulled her to him in a rough embrace, wiping the grin from her face and causing her to stumble against him. Flush against him.

Her hands landed on his chest where dirt now soiled his coat. At this rate, she wouldn't have soiled hands much longer. Not if he insisted on using his person to clean her hands.

"What do you think you are doing?" she asked, her eyes widening as she registered the intent in his eyes. He didn't need to answer her question, because she knew in the tightening of his jawline and the lowering of his mouth that he would kiss her.

He paused his descent to answer her ridiculous question. "I am going to kiss you now."

Her lips parted in anticipation. Her heart quickened to the same rate it reached when she went for a long walk uphill.

And then, a voice carried through the sunny morning air and halted all amorous progress. "Alexandra Emmaline Farris! What in heaven's name are you doing?"

Alexa sprang back at the shrill sound of her mother's voice and muttered a curse. She had come so close to a kiss she should never have welcomed. Now, she didn't even get to experience it.

Lord Collins cleared his throat and smoothed his features into a welcoming smile. "Why Lady Farris, what a delight to see you this morning."

Lady Farris strode toward them with an angry set to her lips. Despite her diminutive size, she appeared quite formidable. Her blue eyes flashed as though the heavens had opened to unleash all its rage while her steps came in jolting, angry strides. "Both of you need to get cleaned up. Immediately." She turned to Lord Collins and thrust a hand on her hip. "And did my eyes deceive me, or were you two locked in an embrace? In the middle of the day? In my garden?"

Alexa gulped, and her face paled. If she were ruined from such a foolish moment as this, she would hate herself forever. She scrambled to come up with an excuse, and she finally managed to say, "We were not locked in an embrace, Mother. I was trying to remove a spider from Lord Collins's person."

She turned to Maxon and raised an expectant eyebrow at him. He shot her a grin and then did nothing. In fact, less than nothing. He stood in place as if he had turned into some sort of statue, rooted immobile on his dais that no mere mortal could reach. "Lord Collins," Alexa hissed at him. She hadn't the faintest idea what had overtaken him. He could not wish to marry her, yet he failed to refute her mother's claims the way any confirmed bachelor ought.

The sun beat down on her without mercy, and the

droplet of sweat that ran down her cheek stood as proof of the heat of the day. She wiped her cheek and scowled when his eyes narrowed on her. An amused gleam entered his otherwise immobile visage, and her scowl intensified. She had forgotten the dirt on her hands. She must have smeared it all over her face just as she had done when she "complimented" Lord Collins.

"If Lord Collins does not wish to say anything, I can at least show you proof, Mother." Alexa stepped in front of Lord Collins and ignored the way her body sang to be near his. "My handprint is on his face. That is where the spider was."

"What did you do? Slap the spider off him?" Lady Farris moved closer to inspect Lord Collins. She exhaled her disappointment. Why, it almost seemed her mother hoped Lord Collins had ruined her only daughter.

Still, Lord Collins remained immobile. And silent. If Alexa lived to one hundred, she would never understand his actions in this moment. He should have vehemently refuted the idea that he could have ruined Alexa, and it irritated her to no end that he did nothing.

Alexa did not resort to violence often, but she would relish fulfilling her next suggestion. "You sound skeptical, Mother. Would you care for a demonstration of how I removed the spider from his person?" To her own ears, her voice sounded anticipatory. Imagine how it must sound to these two around her.

Finally, Lord Collins moved. He coughed and smiled to Alexa, but his eyes held a promise. There would be more to come later. "I am afraid that will not be necessary. I am sure Lady Farris would agree nothing untoward happened here."

Lady Farris's gaze darted from Alexa and then to Lord Collins. Her shoulders slumped in defeat. "Yes, I suppose you are correct." She shook her head and turned back to the manor. "I should know better than to get my hopes up." Her skirts rustled as she moved across the green lawn. "I suggest you both clean up. You two look as though you'd been rolling in the mud."

"Of course, Mother." Alexa moved to follow her mother indoors when Maxon's hand shot out to intercept her.

"Running away so soon?"

Goose bumps sprang to life on her arm, and she whirled to face him. "I am not running. I just think it best I do not stay with someone uninterested in self-preservation. What were you thinking? Did you not care if we were forced to wed?"

"Of course I care."

"You could have fooled me." She shook his hand from her arm and stepped away from him in the direction of the house. She turned to look over her shoulder and said, "It might appear inconceivable, but Mother would happily force you to wed me. Next time, at least try to come up with an excuse for your actions." And, please, please let her know what that excuse is. Because she would dearly like to know.

Chapter 19

Next time. Yes, next time would certainly happen. "You think your mother is the only one who wishes to see us wed?" he muttered as he watched her receding back. She disappeared into the house, and he ran a frustrated hand through his hair. Part of him had hoped Lady Farris would demand he do the honorable thing and marry her daughter, but she had been easily diverted. His own stupidity had convinced him to try and kiss Alexa in broad daylight, in front of multiple windows.

The sun had warmed him to the point of discomfort, and he strode forward. Alexa might behave feistily toward him, but deep down, she desired him. Just as he desired her. The more he thought of her surrounded by her plants, the more his thoughts turned to how delectable she would look at his estate, in his gardens, and more importantly, in his bed.

He took his time returning to the manor, instead choosing to engage in a quiet stroll through the gardens. Her gardens. The clean, even rows of plants looked neat and tidy, without a weed in sight. After one final turn, his hand went to his cheek, and he almost laughed out loud at the dirt caked there. He allowed a small smile to play across his lips as he returned indoors. His steps took him past the library where he couldn't help but overhear the conversation within.

"You say he was in the gardens, helping her weed?" That distinct voice could belong to none other than Gavin.

"Yes," a lyrical voice answered, which Maxon could only assume belonged to the new Lady Farris.

"Do neither of them realize there are servants for that?"

"I suppose not, my love."

He continued on his way to his room, his small smile turning into a grin at the overheard conversation. He had acted in an unusual fashion, but he would not trade his encounter with her for the world.

He strode into his chambers, and Chaney greeted him. "I see your visit has already had a positive effect on your countenance."

Maxon's grin faded, but the spring in his step remained. He was happy.

Chaney hurried to help him change, all the while chatting away. "If I may be so bold as to ask, my lord, what is the reason for your good humor?"

"I think you already know." He had realized long ago that his servants knew all, even if he tried to hide things from them. They had eyes, and ears, everywhere.

"Does it have something to do with Miss Farris?" Chaney asked as he pulled first one boot, then the other, off Maxon's feet.

Chaney confirmed Maxon's belief. He only kept servants he could trust, but it would not do to confide in them. Still, he could not speak to Gavin about his feelings, so Chaney would have to suffice. He needed to speak to someone. Anyone.

"This never leaves this room."

Chaney nodded as he kept his attention riveted on

the task of undressing Maxon.

"Very well, yes. I am afraid it has everything to do with Miss Farris. She would make an ideal countess, do you not agree?"

Of course Chaney must agree and proceeded to do so with an enthusiastic nod.

Maxon frowned and said, "I am afraid it cannot work. Lord Farris would never countenance such a match."

Maxon shed the final remnants of his clothing and went to the tub in the corner as Chaney said, "I expected you earlier, my lord. Would you like me to call for hot water so your bath will be warm?"

"No." He could do with a cold bath. He sank into the lukewarm water and almost submerged himself when he remembered his cheek. He hated to wash away the dirt left by her. Her hand had caressed him there, of her own volition, and now, he sounded like a lovesick fool.

"Have you asked Lord Farris? I cannot imagine anyone would decline your suit, my lord."

Maxon sank lower into the tub. Chaney would not give him an honest answer, at least if the truth hurt at all. Either way, Chaney's words did have their appeal. He could ask Gavin, and if Gavin said no, well, he would figure that out later. What was the worst that could happen? Their friendship could end in ruin, or Gavin might call him out if he thought Maxon had touched his little sister, but Gavin might just say yes.

If Maxon stood in Gavin's shoes, he would prefer to receive an offer rather than hear of some bit of scandal such as an elopement. His friend deserved honesty, and Maxon respected him too much to do otherwise. Yes, he would ask and deal with the consequences later. Of course, he should ascertain Alexa's feelings first.

He ducked his head under the water, scrubbed his cheek, and then emerged from the tub. Toweling dry, he tugged on his smalls and then allowed Chaney to help him with the rest of his clothing. He would find the perfect moment to speak with Alexa, and then he would look for some sign to indicate how she felt. Only then would he seek out her brother.

"Thank you for your advice." He placed his silver watch in his pocket and turned to Chaney. "I shall take your opinion into account."

"Of course, my lord. We all wish to see you happy."

Maxon smiled and departed the room. He may as well begin his wooing endeavors now, assuming he could find her. He strode down the hallway and into the library. There, Gavin and Laura reclined on a settee. On further examination, Maxon could hear the faintest of snores as Lady Farris slept, nestled in Gavin's arms.

"Her delicate condition has made her unusually tired," Gavin whispered by way of explanation.

"Of course." As a gentleman, Maxon would not point out the lady's embarrassing behavior, no matter how noteworthy.

"She never snored, not until after we discovered she was increasing." Gavin smiled a tender smile as he smoothed Laura's hair back.

"How fortunate for you."

Gavin chuckled, indicating a chair to his right. Maxon took the proffered seat as Gavin asked, "Will you attend the race without me, then?"

"I think not." Such an endeavor held no appeal, seeing as Alexa would not attend.

"Are you certain? I shan't hold it against you, you know." Gavin shook his head, grimaced, and said, "If only that infernal letter had not been lost in the post."

"Indeed."

"Of course, you could return home. You don't live that far away."

A louder snore filled the room, and Laura shifted. Her eyes opened, and she gazed up into her husband's eyes with a loving smile on her face. "Did I nod off?"

"Yes, but I, your valiant knight, protected you as you slumbered." Gavin bent to kiss his wife, and Maxon rose from his chair.

Neither noticed Maxon as he departed the room. He could have stayed, but Gavin would prefer his absence, just as Maxon did. Such a sight was not for his eyes.

****

Alexa brushed her mare's coat with strong strokes, attempting to block out thoughts of Maxon with physical activity. While she preferred gardening, the midday sun shone too hot and strong. If she wished to avoid a megrim, she needed to stay indoors.

"He is infuriating, you know," she whispered to her mare. The horse's ear twitched at the sound, and Alexa continued to speak in soothing tones. "I cannot understand him. His actions are those of a bedlamite." She stopped brushing to push back a strand of her own hair, and then returned to her work. "Can you believe he desired compliments? *Him*?"

She *tsk*ed and moved down to address her mare's flanks. "Of course I gave him one." She let out a heartfelt sigh and shook her head. "But for what purpose? So he may tease me? I cannot understand him."

Her mare shifted and gave a soft neigh in response, just as footsteps filled the stable. Alexa did not desire to deal with people and ducked down in the corner of the stall. The footsteps drew nearer, and she sucked in her breath. She overreacted, but Maxon might linger just outside the door, and she couldn't see him. Not now.

The footsteps stopped in front of her stall, and she crouched lower. Her mare tilted her head and looked at Alexa with curious eyes. Even the horse thought her actions strange.

"What are you doing down there?"

Alexa jumped into a standing position as Maxon joined her in the little stall. Of course, he would find her stooped like that. "Is it not obvious?" She very well could bluff him into believing her behavior normal. Maybe.

"I fear not."

"Hmm." She smiled and stepped to her mare's buttock, past him where a shimmer of awareness tickled her senses. She resumed her brushing as if nothing amiss had transpired. "What are you doing here?"

"I came to find you."

Her brush stopped midstroke as she craned her head to look at him. Why ever should he look for her? Oh yes. Her stomach plummeted. He promised their little tête-à-tête would resume at a later time, which must mean now.

"How did you know to find me here?"

He leaned against the doorway, filling her only exit with his large frame and winsome smile. She returned her attention to her horse. Why exactly did he wish to speak with her? Never before had he searched her out to tease her.

"Your hat and gloves are outside the stall on a bale of hay."

How had she forgotten that minor detail? And more importantly, how long had he searched before coming to the stables? His behavior was decidedly odd.

Placing her hand on the rump of her mare, she crossed behind and resumed her work, this time facing Maxon where she did not feel quite as vulnerable. Of course, she had to look at him, but now a horse separated them.

"You said I look better clean. Well, how do I look now?" He grinned, turning his head from side to side while keeping his gaze planted on her.

"Fine." She shrugged. A momentary flash of something undefinable passed through his eyes. She dropped her gaze, allowing her brushstrokes to monopolize her attention. Her bravado could only last for so long, especially when faced with this handsome man.

"Yes, well, you look delightful today. Did I mention that earlier?"

"You did not." She tried to sound prim, but her voice came out breathless, much to her chagrin.

He stepped from his reclined position and stopped when he reached her mare. Of course, a horse separated them, but horses were rather mobile creatures, and Alexa did not feel safe. Not at all.

"I should have." His voice came out in a low whisper, and his eyes grew earnest. "How can I make up for my grievous error?"

Avoiding eye contact as much as possible, she moved down her mare to continue her brushing. Thank heavens she had a diversion from him. Otherwise, his interest alone would have ignited her in a burst of flames. "No error has occurred, my lord."

He shook his head with a scowl on his lips. "I fear there have been too many errors committed as of late."

Whatever could he mean by that? How should she deal with such a statement? Brushing with renewed vigor, she hurried to the rump. She needed to finish her ministrations so she could leave.

"Stroll with me, Alexa."

His request sounded innocent, except for the definite gleam of something more in his eyes which betrayed his mischievous intent. She gulped and dropped her gaze. Her pulse raced at the thought of strolling with him, and she blushed.

Botheration. Yes, she would stroll with him. She could not lie to herself and tell herself otherwise. "If you insist."

"I do." He placed his hand on the hindquarters of the mare and crossed to her side. Taking her hand in his, he drew her out of the stall and into the aisle. She stopped before the hay bale and exchanged her brush for her hat and gloves.

"You know, Tyr is a couple stalls down from here. If you wish to employ your expert brushing techniques on him, feel free."

She glowered at him, not deigning to respond, instead turning to walk unhindered out of the stables. He caught her elbow and pulled her to a stop, not near enough to the exit to please her. She kept her back ramrod straight, but the shiver of anticipation running up her spine betrayed her appreciation of his presence.

"You know, we never did determine if your hair color matched Tyr's."

Something within her snapped. Her rational side that knew he teased her disappeared with an internal splintering, falling away for reclamation at a later time. She would never accept someone comparing her to a horse. Never.

"Have you gone mad?" she hissed, clenching her hands into fists and turning to face him. His eyes glinted with wicked amusement, and she squinted as her ire increased. Ever since his return to London, he had behaved increasingly oddly, but did he ever explain himself? No.

She stepped forward until she stood almost toe to toe with him and pointed her index finger at him. "I tolerated your presence in London and at Nettleridge, but I shan't tolerate it any longer. You with your inscrutable motives and irrational actions can go hang for all I care. Just leave me alone."

"Did you truly find my motives inscrutable?"

His countenance darkened, and her thoughts tangled in bewilderment. "Of course I did." One did not demand she not marry another, then treat her with the utmost respect, then almost kiss her in the gardens. What part of that was supposed to be comprehensible?

"Alexandra." He *tsk*ed. "Sweet, sweet Alexandra." He brought his hand to caress her cheek, stroking her skin as if to calm her as he would a horse. "Something has brewed between us for some time now."

Her ire doused instantly. She could only stare at him. "Really?" Something brewed between them? Of course she felt something brewing, but did he feel the same thing she felt?

"Yes," he murmured. His eyes held her with their intensity. Too much intensity. She gulped and swayed, but he held her in place with an amused frown. "Are your nerves affecting you, again?"

Obtuse man. He knew what he did to her. "No."

"Then what is the matter? Are your feelings for me getting to you?"

She squeaked. He knew. He knew her heart beat for him and him alone. His hand moved down her arm, lowering her forgotten pointed index finger and capturing her hand in his. "You said something back at Nettleridge. Something I cannot seem to forget."

"Oh?" Heavens, how had she lost her ability to speak?

"Yes. When we sat together on that bench as the sun dipped below the skyline, you claimed I would run from you if you professed some grand love for me." He shifted, his eyes going to linger on her lips. "I would never run from you. Never. Not even if you keep up this charade of disliking me."

"Charade?" What did he refer to now? Come to think of it, she might have mentioned she didn't like him back in London, and a few times after, but that happened ages ago.

"Yes. I know you don't dislike me. In fact, I think you like me very much."

"You make it sound like you prefer me to hold some grand love for you." He couldn't, though. His ego might have grown larger than most, but he wouldn't stoop to cruelty to fuel his self-image. She would never believe that of him.

"Well, yes, I do prefer that." His lips twitched, and

her jaw dropped.

She tore her hand from his. Why did she stand so near to him? Backing away from him, she said, "I suppose I don't *dis*like you."

"Come now. You can do better than that," he said as he stepped forward.

"Would you prefer to hear me say I like you?" She took another step, adding yet another for good measure.

In answer, he took two steps forward, although his steps must cover more distance than hers. Now he almost stood flush with her. "No." His arm snaked around her waist, and she found herself in the same embrace she had escaped from earlier. Except this time, she smelled of horses and the outdoors, and he smelled clean and minty. "I would prefer to hear you say you love me."

She clamped her lips together, lest her jaw drop again. Why would he want to hear her say that? Well, no matter his logic, she wouldn't. So, she raised her brow and said, "Fine. You love me. Happy now?"

His eyelids lowered and he said in a low rumble, "How amusing." Except he didn't sound amused. He sounded fraught with danger. "Now that you've guessed how I feel, I need to know if you feel the same."

Shock made her mind draw a blank. If someone had informed her of a fire in the manor, she would have felt less surprise. "Y-you love me?"

"Of course I do. Why else would I come here?"

"For the Almhurst race."

"Alexa." He *tsk*ed. "I don't live far enough away for that to be a logical excuse."

"Then why are you here?" If her brain functioned

correctly, she could make sense of this. His sheer nearness did not allow for normalcy, though. So she would have to settle for slowly connecting the dots.

"I am here for you. To hold you, kiss you, make you love me." Her lips parted, and he shrugged. "If you will not say you love me, then I might as well see to the other part of my quest."

He lowered his lips to hers, and this time, no outside force conspired against them. His lips felt hungry against hers, or thirsty, or...oh drat. She could not decide. Not when his tongue met hers, and she melted against him. Who cared how he seemed, except he held her, kissed her, and said he loved her?

Her girlhood dream had come true. Every ounce of his lithe frame suggested it. Her hand flew to his hair, while the other examined his hard back. Every inch of it.

He growled into her and started making movements of his own. Starting with her hair, he found a few pins and tossed them aside. Now, half her hair spilled down her back. He drew back long enough to look at her and smile. "Your hair makes me lose myself."

He didn't wait for a response. Instead, he resumed their kiss, allowing his free hand to skim down her back until it met her buttocks. He growled again as he squeezed, and her worries that he might not approve of her curves fell to the wayside, forgotten. He most definitely approved.

The most alarming tingles flew about inside her, unchecked except they all seemed to pool inside of her, forming into a tight ball of wanting she never would have expected. She needed him to touch her, to hold her much tighter. Anything to stave off this building tension.

His lips trailed down her neck, and that tension increased. She did not know how much more she could take without betraying herself to him, if she hadn't already.

He nipped at her collarbone, and she moaned. There. She had betrayed herself.

He chuckled, his hand on her bottom pulling her harder against him. "Well, Alexandra, do you love me? Or will I have to leave with a broken heart, my mission unfulfilled?"

He made another teasing little nip on her collarbone, and she shuddered. Her eyes clenched tight, and she nodded. Pleasure racked her as he returned to kissing her.

"I couldn't hear you, love."

"I love you," she whispered, resuming their kiss with an unexpected fervor. He smiled against her and slowly untangled himself. With one final kiss, he broke away, separating from her and replacing his warmth with cold, empty air.

"Oh, my dear…" His voice sounded jubilant, and she opened her eyes to find an equally happy smile. "That is all I needed to hear." He tidied his hair in one sweep and pulled his jacket into place. He looked perfect.

"If you will excuse me, I must go see your brother." He grinned at her, and then stepped past her to the door. With one final glance behind him, he left the stables, his feet crunching against the gravel with each receding step.

The stable door slammed behind him, and her jaw

dropped. Where was he going? She longed to run after him, to ask what in the devil he was thinking, leaving her here like this, but she needed to fix her hair and dress. But really, what in the devil was he thinking? The day had turned into a whirlwind, but the one thing she knew—Maxon *loved* her. He loved her!

She stooped down to pick up her hair pins, as well as her forgotten accessories. Tidying her hair into a quick bun, she strolled back to the hay bale and dumped her hat and gloves down. Her mare needed a much more thorough brushing.

Chapter 20

Maxon pushed the front door open, his purposeful steps eating up the distance to wherever Gavin might be. He would check the library first, and then continue through the house until he located his friend. He would find him. He must. After all, he had received the response he sought from Alexa.

His smile of happiness refused to leave his face, even after he checked the library and found no traces of either Gavin or Laura. Turning back into the hall, he strode toward the parlor but stopped short before colliding with Gavin.

"Aren't we in a rush?" Gavin asked with a quizzical expression.

"As a matter of fact, I am. I must speak to you. In private."

"Oh? You might as well accompany me to the library. I must fetch a book for Laura."

Turning, Maxon joined him for the short walk. He did not speak, not until they reached their destination and Maxon verified they could converse without curious listeners.

Gavin stopped before the rows of books, which spanned from floor to ceiling, and eyed the volumes before him. "Well, what is it?"

Maxon took a seat on a velvet armchair as an unusual feeling of worry descended. He prided himself on his behavior as a gentleman, and this next conversation reaffirmed his belief in himself. A gentleman did not betray his friends and engaged in only the most honorable of endeavors. No matter what happened here, he would uphold his standards.

"I have fallen for someone."

Gavin pulled a book from the shelf but, at Maxon's words, stopped all movement. He craned his head to view Maxon and asked, "What? Who?"

Now was the moment. The moment to be brave. He squared his shoulders and said, "Your sister."

The harsh sound of silence filled the air as Gavin stared at him. "Who?"

"Alexa."

Gavin's eyes narrowed on Maxon, before smiling a grim smile. "I think not."

****

Alexa had brushed her mare in a frenzied manner, unable to get Maxon out of her mind. He had seemed almost on a mission. First, he found her here in the stables. Then, he kissed a confession of her feelings out of her. Lastly, once he heard her confession, he left. She had little experience with love, but something seemed off. And now, she could not focus on her mare.

She snared her hat and gloves from the bale of hay, not bothering to put them on as she trudged back to the house. The heat of the day left her feeling quite parched, and she longed for a good cup of tea. Yes, she would have some tea sent to her room, right after she procured a torrid romance novel of Laura's. Nothing else would hold her interest now.

Her feet beat a silent path to the library, but she stopped when angry voices filled the hallway, practically beckoning Alexa to eavesdrop. Especially when she recognized the voices as Maxon's and Gavin's.

She inched nearer to the doorframe and pressed herself against the wall in order to hear the conversation within. If anyone other than Maxon spoke in the library, she would never dream of eavesdropping…again, but she needed insight into his thinking, and this might help.

"You will never be good enough for her."

Long silence filled the corridor, until the scraping of a chair on the floor filled the void. "You know there could be no better suitor than I."

Alexa's breath caught at Maxon's words, and she pressed flush against the cold, hard wall. Did they speak of her? If Maxon had kissed her minutes before and now spoke of another lady, she would…well, she would never speak to him again.

Gavin's voice drifted to her, his words a mixture of anger and frustration. "You don't love her. For all I know, you still hold a torch for Miss Ashford."

"Of course not," Maxon said in a passionate outburst. "I have come to understand I could never love a woman I did not know. I loved an illusion, but illusions fade once one sees the truth."

A long moment of silence ensued, and Alexa shut her eyes, trying her best to imagine the scene inside. Gavin would never get upset with his best friend, unless they did speak of her. It was the only logical conclusion she could form.

Gavin sounded tired as he exhaled. "She deserves far better than you."

"Who do you suggest she marry, then?" When

Gavin failed to respond, Maxon said, "I wished to do the honorable thing and speak with you before her. I implore you to at least contemplate the matter."

"I will not." Gavin gave a harsh laugh. "You may pack your things and leave."

More silence followed, and she shuddered at the terrible note of anger in Gavin's voice. What could she do to help the situation? Why, Maxon intended to ask for her hand. She should help in some way.

A noise sounded from the library, and Alexa awoke from her thoughts. She turned to rush down the hall before someone caught her. She managed two steps before a firm hand grasped her elbow and turned her around.

"You have a knack for eavesdropping on unfortunate conversations, my dear."

Alexa brought her gaze to Maxon's, and she trembled at the light in those blue eyes. A dark cast tinged their light shade, one that did not bode well.

She mustered her courage and smiled at him. "How am I to discern your motives without eavesdropping?"

"By asking me." He dropped his hand to hers and pulled her a step nearer to him.

"What am I supposed to ask? Why did you demand my compliments? Why did you kiss me? Why do you speak of marriage to my brother?" She shook her head. He never gave her the chance to ask the pertinent questions. "You do too many odd things to question them all."

"Do I?" His finger brushed her lips as his eyes pierced her. "Name one."

"Aside from what I just asked?" He nodded, and she said darkly, "You said you loved me." There. That

241

was the most unusual thing he had done. How could someone like him, come to love someone like her? She spent too much time entrenched in dirt, too far below his standards.

His eyes flashed with unspoken feelings of anger and question. "You don't know your own worth. How could I not love you?"

The sound of a chair scraping against the library floor made him start, and his eyes narrowed on her. "Are there other odd things you wish to question?"

"Of course," she breathed. She could not name any at the moment, but she would, given time.

"Right. Well, I will rectify my error. And now, forgive me for my lapse of gentlemanly behavior. Some things warrant unscrupulous actions." His other hand went around her waist, and she shivered at the intimate touch.

"Such as?"

He smirked. "Such as taking this tumble together." His lips descended on hers, freezing any additional questions she might have on her tongue. She could feel his heart beating at a frenzied pace as he pulled her flush against him. Not the same sort of pace as earlier. This raced faster, harder.

His heart matched the voracity of his kiss. He consumed her in a rush, leaving her breathless, holding on to his lapels for dear life.

The faintest of sounds invaded her senses, and she remembered herself. She tried to break away, but he whispered, "Trust me, my love," before kissing her once more.

Her heart stuttered to hear those words, and she nodded against him. She could feel his lips curl in a smile, just as a loud shriek filled the hallway.

"What are you doing?"

True panic set in as the dowager Lady Farris's voice echoed down the lengthy hallway. Alexa would trust Maxon, even as her fate seemed to veer toward ruination.

Maxon pulled them to a straightened position and turned to face her mother. "Lady Farris," he said with a bow as he disengaged from Alexa, except for the hand which still held hers. "Your daughter has just agreed to become my wife."

Alexa's head spun with the day's events. According to Maxon, they were engaged, but had he asked her? No.

"What goes on here?" Alexa turned to find Gavin as he rushed from the library. His eyes appeared wild as he found Alexa and Maxon together, and he took a threatening step toward Maxon. "I told you to leave."

"Now, now, Gavin," Lady Farris said in a soothing whisper. "Congratulations are in order. Lord Collins and Alexandra shall wed."

"No, they shall not."

"And why not?" Alexa's mother asked with raised brow and commanding tone as she strode forward, stopping in front of Gavin with a fierce frown.

Suddenly, Gavin did not look as sure of himself, but he still said in clipped tones, "I said so."

"That may be, but you did not see how Lord Collins was ravishing Alexa moments before."

"What?" Gavin asked, his voice a loud angry roar. He clenched his hands together in fists and eyed Maxon with a wary frown before turning to his mother. "He could not have ravished her. I spoke with him minutes before you found them."

"I found them in a most compromising position, Gavin."

Gavin's jaw clenched, and he turned to Alexa. "Tell Mother you have not been ravished."

Alexa opened her mouth to speak, but Maxon shook his head. "Your sister is ruined. We shall wed immediately."

"And I say there was no time."

"Really? Both your mother and I claim she is compromised. Why do you wish condemnation on your sister?"

"Yes, Gavin. Let it rest." Alexa turned to her mother, as her mother's eyes lit with a gleam of happiness. Her mother extended her hand, and Alexa accepted as Lady Farris said, "Now then, Alexa and I shall leave you two to discuss the matter." Her eyes hardened, and she said, "Behave yourselves." Then, she led Alexa down the hall, away from her betrothed. Her very new, very surprising betrothed.

****

Silence descended as the ladies departed, until Gavin cleared his throat and said, "Well, we might as well have a drink."

They returned to the library where Gavin poured himself scotch, leaving Maxon to fend for himself. He poured a couple fingers into a crystal glass, and then sat in the chair across from Gavin, who appeared ready to throttle him.

"I am sorry." Gavin would never accept his apology, and rightly so. Maxon had sworn to act the gentleman, yet done the complete opposite at the first opportunity. What mattered more though? To keep his friendship with Gavin, or to marry the woman he loved? The same woman who loved him in return?

"Your apology matters little. I can only assume you tricked Alexa into marrying you, and now she has no choice but to. Even if your honor means little, I shall see you two wed."

Maxon lounged back in his chair, crossing his booted feet in front of him. The idea that he would marry Alexa sank in, and with it, a happy and relaxed mood. Even if his best friend wished him bodily harm, Maxon could rest easy knowing she loved him. She loved him. He smiled, until he remembered his situation. Sure enough, Gavin's eyes rested on him with a blazing look of fury, and Maxon wiped the smile from his face.

"You know I did not trick her, and I tried to gain your permission before speaking with her." He exhaled and took a sip of his scotch. "Sometimes you are too hard-headed for your own good."

"Am I?" Gavin swirled the contents of his glass in a lazy circle as he examined the amber liquid. He heaved a heavy sigh and set the glass on his desk. "You know you will provide a generous amount of pin money for her, and upon your death, will ensure she is well cared for."

"Of course. I shall have my solicitor draw up the necessary paperwork."

"And the Almhurst race is out of the question. You will wed Alexa, and forego such foolish diversions."

At this, Maxon could not help but snicker. Gavin's eyes narrowed in a frosty stare and he said, "You bloody bastard. I should have guessed you were not here for the race. I thought your excuse to linger rather than return home a bit off."

"Isn't it normal to ensure one's best friend is enjoying marriage?" Come to think of it, if Gavin returned the favor and visited shortly after Maxon married Alexa, Maxon would be annoyed in the extreme.

"No," Gavin said without an ounce of humor. "Was my letter even lost?"

Maxon shrugged, and muttered, "I may have used that as my excuse to see your sister."

"Of course you did." Gavin shuddered. "You did not waste much time compromising her, did you?" He threw back the remainder of his drink. Maxon stood, procured the bottle of scotch, and poured another glass for Gavin.

As he returned to his chair he said, "For what it is worth, I did not plan it. She sort of presented herself at the ideal moment." And she had. Even now his pulse accelerated in remembrance of spotting her the moment he left the library. Her eyes had turned their typical thunderstormy hue, and he knew the moment had arrived for him to further his suit. When else would he be presented with such an ideal opportunity?

"Yes, Alexa would." Gavin shook his head, a momentary smile tugging up his lips.

Relief thumped in Maxon's chest. Perhaps they could salvage their friendship. "And can you blame me? You would have done the same thing for your Laura."

"True enough." Gavin reached over, picked up his newly filled glass, and downed it. He set the glass down once more and smirked. "You had best hurry. I expect you to return in no less than a week with your special license."

He moved away from the desk, to the door, and Maxon called after him, "I thought Laura required a book?"

Gavin turned with a pained frown. "She will enjoy hearing of the day's events much more, I think."

Maxon chuckled as his friend departed. He stood, and placed his empty glass next to Gavin's. He ought to depart for London straightaway, but first he needed to find Alexa.

****

The door clicked shut behind Alexa, and she crossed to sit on her bed. Her mother already had the doors to Alexa's armoire open and examined the clothing held within. "There is no time. You will need constant attention to get your trousseau ready before the wedding." Her mother *tsk*ed and shut the doors. "Why, you have two worn nightgowns and nothing more. It is shameful."

Alexa had never worried about her nightgowns, but now the implications of such garments hit her. Maxon would see her, all of her, and not just in the odd chance he happened into her room as he did at the house party. The notion that she should marry soon had not sunk in yet, but then, how did one expect such a realization when she had not even received an offer of marriage?

Concern filled her mother's eyes as she crossed to sit beside Alexa. "You are happy, aren't you? If you don't wish to marry him, I am certain we can figure something out." Her voice trailed off in a sad whisper, ending in silence too difficult to countenance.

The thought of not marrying him sent a wave of panic tearing through her. "Of course I wish to marry him. Don't buy me a cottage by the sea yet, Mother. I will not turn into a ruined spinster."

"Oh, marvelous." Her mother smiled and turned to Alexa. "I always hoped for a love match for you…You do love him, don't you?"

Now this, this Alexa could answer with certainty. "Yes, Mother. I love him." She ducked her head as her cheeks heated. So long as she understood she loved Maxon, the rest would fall into place, assuming his feelings held fast, of course.

"Marvelous." Her mother stood and beamed at her as she clapped her hands together. "I shall send for the village seamstress. We have much to do in too little time." She paused as she reached the door and turned to Alexa once more. "I am so very proud of you, dearest. No better match could have been made, much less as a love match." She sighed and left Alexa to her musings with only the barest of sounds to indicate her departure.

Alexa stood and paced her room. Who would have guessed her life could alter so drastically without her verbal consent? Of course, she could not grow angry with Maxon. She had allowed him to kiss her, even after she thought to discontinue the kiss, which must mean some sort of consent. She scowled as she stopped her pacing. Botheration. She needed to see him.

She left her room and went downstairs.

She descended the wide staircase but stopped halfway down. Maxon stood beneath, waiting for her with his winsome smile. She resumed her descent, and he bowed as she reached him. "My lady," he said, offering his hand. "Would you care to stroll with me?"

She placed her hand in his, and asked, "Is this the stroll you promised me earlier?"

"If you wish." He grinned and tucked her arm in his. They stepped outside into the warmth of the sun, and she inhaled deeply. The scent of lilies beckoned to her, even overpowering his minty scent. And taste. She would never forget the taste of him. He tasted of pure nectar.

After a few short steps, she whirled to face him. They stood in the cobbled drive, with the rolling green lawn stretched before them. The sunny day and the excellent view could not hold her attention, as she could not stand this infernal torment any longer. "I have questions for you. As usual, your behavior is odd, and I think I have the right to know what you are about."

"I thought my behavior most sensible. I wish to marry you."

"I gathered as much." She fought down the melting feeling in her chest and squared her shoulders. "When did you decide this?"

"About a week ago."

He was not very forthcoming with his answers. Of course, he had answered her question, but this conversation would take all day if she had to ask for every detail, one at a time. She raised her brow and placed her hands on her hips, hoping he would understand he needed to continue. Of course, he did not, so she asked, "Well? Can you not explain your actions?"

"Of course I can." He swept a hand through his hair, and her stomach flopped when the blond locks fell in a splendid picture of disarray. He pulled her to the stone step leading to the entrance of the house and sat with her, keeping her hand in his. "I fell in love with you, my dear, but you told me you disliked me. I could not bring myself to believe you and decided to come here and ascertain the truth of the matter, allowing you to either break my heart or encourage it."

Again, her heart melted, but this time she allowed it to pool inside of her chest in its little puddle. How could she not? The man she always hoped for, nay, always could not hope for, had handed his heart to her. His eyes held hers, and she prompted, "And?"

"And you confessed to love me, so I went to secure Gavin's blessing. He refused me, and ordered me away."

Of course Gavin would act the protective boor.

"Then, I entered the hallway to find you there. I knew Gavin would leave the library and decided to force his compliance, as long as you loved me. Only then would the forfeiture of such a lengthy friendship be worthwhile." He shook his head as a gleam of mirth entered his eyes and said, "Of course, I never thought your mother would happen upon us."

Alexa exhaled. Everything he said sounded magical, even if she had not received an offer of marriage. What Maxon had endured was far more noteworthy than kneeling and asking her a simple question. "So you truly wish to marry me?" Even if he did not ask, she had to hear him say it.

"Yes, my love. This past week has been torture without you. I need you with me, and as long as you love me and wish to marry me, I could not ask for any greater boon than to have you as my wife."

Their eyes locked, and a gust of wind dislodged several tendrils of her hair, causing them to play across her face. Those stray strands tickled, but she could not tear herself from that shared moment of silence, especially when his head lowered and his lips caught hers in a warm embrace.

"I thought I told you to leave."

Their lips had touched for the briefest of moments when Gavin's voice split the stillness. Alexa jumped back and craned her neck to find the source of the sound. On the second floor, an open window allowed Gavin to glare down on them. His comical frown, coupled with her sheer joy from the day's events, caused Alexa to break into laughter. She could not help herself.

Gavin continued to frown, and he shook his head. "Alexa, get inside, and Maxon, hurry up and leave already. You may kiss her when you wed her." Then, he shut the window.

Of course, he watched from above, so Alexa wiped away the tears from her eyes and smiled at Maxon as she rose. "I fear I must go. I wish you a safe journey, my love." Turning on her heel to hide the blush on her face, she rushed inside without once looking back. Why look back, when soon enough, she could look on his handsome face every day for the rest of her life?

Chapter 21

"I cannot understand why this wedding must take place so soon after Lord Collins's return," Alexa said as Laura joined her in her chambers. The tea had arrived a short while earlier, and Alexa had already downed her first cup.

She had awoken to a shock when her maid arrived bright and early that morning, urging her to get up and prepare for her wedding. At first, she assumed someone tried to make some grand jest at her expense, but no. Her wedding would transpire that morning.

Laura cocked her head to the side as she sat down on an armchair. She glowed with impending motherhood, although her waist had barely begun to thicken. Pouring herself a cup of tea, she tilted her head to the side and asked, "Do you not wish to marry him?"

"Of course, but he only returned last night!"

"Yes, well, Gavin joked this hasty wedding was his gift to your betrothed."

Alexa's brow drew together in confusion. No one would return from a strenuous trip to London and get married the very next morning. Why, he must be exhausted. Wouldn't Maxon prefer a few days rest first? Unless…she blushed. Maybe that was what Gavin meant by that jest. The wedding night. "I thought Gavin did not want me to marry his best friend."

Sipping on her tea, Laura smiled and set the cup on

its saucer. "I believe when his initial surprise wore off, he came around."

A knock sounded on the door, and the dowager Lady Farris entered with a bevy of servants trailing behind her. "We must hurry." She directed several servants to the armoire and then turned back to Alexa. "Your wedding shall commence in two hours. We must hurry." Bringing her hand to her forehead, she paled as she said, "Gavin is cruel. There is simply no time. The wedding breakfast will fall short of the feast you deserve, and what does Gavin say? Nothing. The fiend."

Alexa giggled as Laura said, "His intent is for the bride and groom to skip the wedding breakfast so they may return to Lord Collins's estate."

"What?" Alexa's mother stopped short. She appeared even nearer to swooning. "You mean Alexa will avoid her wedding breakfast, just as you two did?"

"Err yes," Laura said, setting aside her cup and saucer. "Gavin wants them as far from here as possible by nightfall."

Alexa blushed at the implications. Her brother could act in such a foolish manner sometimes. "We will stay for the wedding breakfast. After all, our trip will take less than two hours by carriage."

She rose from her bed and started to draw on her robe but halted as her mother said, "Oh, Alexa, do not bother. We have no time."

She shed the robe and nodded as butterflies overtook her stomach. She would marry today.

****

Alexa settled into the carriage which took her to the little chapel in town. Her long white gloves encased her arms, while her dark locks lay in a mutinous pile of curls on top of her head. Seed pearls nestled in the recesses of her hair matched the seed pearls trimming the décolletage on her otherwise plain ivory gown. The seamstress had worked diligently to compile all the necessary garments for Alexa, and Alexa had no complaints.

"You look beautiful." Her mother smiled across the carriage as it rocked into motion. Tears glistened in the eyes so very much like her own, and Alexa placed a comforting hand on her mother's.

A shared look of love passed between the two, and soon, they arrived at the chapel. A footman helped them down, and her mother left her as Gavin joined her. "Are you sure about this? I can send him away, you know."

Alexa swatted her brother and said, "I do not believe he would agree to that."

"Yes," he said as he considered her with pride shining from his eyes. "I do believe you are correct."

He pulled her into a tight hug and said, "I will miss having you around, which means, if he should mistreat you in any way, you will return here."

"Of course." Her overbearing brother was endearing in moments such as these. In fact, everything seemed better today. Even the overcast skies appeared brighter, and the songbirds louder. Today, she would wed the man she had dreamt of since girlhood. How could this day be anything other than marvelous?

The music started from within, and Gavin smiled down on her. "Shall we?"

"Yes, please."

He nodded and held his arm out to her. Leading her in, she almost stumbled when her eyes met Maxon's.

His navy-blue morning coat, starched cravat, and white breeches looked stunning on him. That and the silver watch fob dangling from his breeches' waistband lent him a look of grandeur. Of course, nothing compared to the look in his eye. The look of joyous rapture at the sight of her. She never thought to feel as beautiful as she did now. He made her feel this way, him and him alone.

Gavin handed her off, and the clergyman launched into a sermon on the benefits of holy matrimony. Alexa could not tear her gaze from Maxon's, not when they exchanged vows, nor when Maxon slipped the ring on her finger. No, she could not tear her gaze from his until he placed the gentlest of kisses on her lips.

"I love you," he breathed, his lips leaving hers.

"And I you," she whispered as her eyes fluttered open. She hovered in a dream right now, and nothing mattered but her love before her.

"Well, then, my countess, shall we?"

She nodded, and they faced the small crowd as the vicar announced the new couple. Her mother cried, and she, along with Gavin and Laura, stood to cheer the newlywed couple as Maxon clasped Alexa's hand in his and pulled his bride down the aisle. She flew with him, right into the waiting carriage.

A footman closed the door, and then the carriage rocked into motion. Maxon turned to her with a smile and nodded at her left hand. "Do you like it?"

She looked down to discover the ring on her finger. A large star sapphire rested on a gold band. No, she did not like it. She adored it. "Very much."

He smiled, but his eyes clouded over as he pulled her near. "I must warn you. Your ring is not made for gardening, and I happen to have a large garden."

Her heart lurched, and she inched nearer so their legs nestled against each other. "Oh? What would you suggest I do, then?"

"First off, remove the thing before you garden."

She scowled. Of course she would remove it first. "And the second?"

He grinned and brought her hand to his mouth. "Who said anything about a second?"

"You implied it, my lord." She frowned. He was exceedingly obtuse again.

"If you insist, I can name a second."

She waited, but all he did was trail kisses up her arm. He scowled and removed the glove from her hand, and then resumed his kisses on the tender inside of her wrist. If she tried really hard, she could still think. Couldn't she? "Yes?" Her voice emerged faint, nearly inaudible.

His lips stilled but lingered just above her. His breath sent hot whispers on the minuscule hairs on her arm, and she shivered from the feeling. "Since you demand there be a second point, I will make it something to my liking." He pulled her off the cushion and onto his lap. Placing a finger on her lips, he trailed his finger down to her chin and onto her chest, until it dipped down to the neckline of her gown, hooking there and lingering to draw her closer. "The second, dearest, is I shall be the only one allowed to place it back on your hand."

She could accept that and would tell him once she regained use of her faculties. He lowered his lips to her neck and kissed her there, his arms holding her within their welcoming confines. "You know, I think you were made to sit just like this. Here, on me."

She blushed. She had forgotten her scandalous position. The thought crossed her mind to remove herself, but instead she tilted her head to allow him more access to her neck. Such kisses could transport her elsewhere, and why fight them? She was his, and he hers. Just as it should be.

A word about the author...

Naomi Boom never expected to love writing. Her inspiration struck when she was searching for the perfect historical romance novel to read. Nothing sounded appealing, so she decided to write her own. That one novel has morphed into a series and hopefully many, many more.

She resides in her home state of South Dakota with her husband and toddler. Her dream is to someday find an acreage where she can raise chickens and continue her writing.

Website: http://www.naomiboom.com
Email: naomi@naomiboom.com
Facebook: http://www.facebook.com/NaomiMBoom/
Twitter: @naomimboom